FRANCIS POULENC

Other works by Richard D. E. Burton

Baudelaire in 1859. A Study in the Sources of Poetic Creativity
(Cambridge U.P., 1988)

Baudelaire and the Second Republic. Writing and Revolution
(Oxford U.P., 1991)

Afro-Creole. Power, Opposition and Play in the Caribbean
(Cornell U.P., 1997)

Blood in the City. Violence and Revelation in Paris, 1789-1945
(Cornell U.P., 2001)

O
Outlines

FRANCIS POULENC

RICHARD D. E. BURTON

Absolute Press

First published in 2002 by

Absolute Press
Scarborough House,
29 James Street West,
Bath, England BA1 2BT
Phone 01225 316013
Fax 01225 445836
E-mail outlines@absolutepress.demon.co.uk

Series editor Nick Drake

Printed by Legoprint, Italy

ISBN 1 899791 09 4

Contents

Acknowledgements   7

Legislation on homosexuality in France   9

'Homosexuel', 'pédéraste', 'inverti', etc.   11

Abbreviations   12

Introduction   13

The Parises of Francis Poulenc   17

The Ox on the Roof: Poulenc, Les Six, and the 1920s   28

Homosexuality, Catholicism and modernism   43

Black Virgin: Poulenc at Rocamadour (August 1936)   61

Faith, death and freedom: Poulenc's music 1937-50   77

Monologues and dialogues: Poulenc's later music 1950-63   90

Conclusion   118

Notes   124

Picture credits   135

Acknowledgements

This book is neither a biography of Poulenc's life nor a critical study of his music as such. The best general account available of Poulenc's life and work is Benjamin Ivry's *Francis Poulenc* (Phaidon Press, 1996), and the most accessible musicological study is Wilfred Mellers's admirable *Francis Poulenc* (Oxford University Press, 1993), much utilised here; a rather more specialised work is Keith W. Daniel's detailed and painstaking *Francis Poulenc. His Artistic Development and Musical Style* (UMI Research Press, 1982), and, in French, Renaud Machart's *Poulenc* (Seuil, 1995) is a first-rate general study and supplants the earlier study by Poulenc's friend, Henri Hell. It was, unfortunately, only after completing my manuscript that I gained access to the valuable collection of essays edited by Sidney Buckland and Myriam Chimènes, *Frances Poulenc. Music, Art and Literature* (Ashgate, 1999). I have decided to leave my original text unchanged, but interested readers are referred to the notes for further discussion of the points I have raised. The primary material for this study is Poulenc's own writings, above all his voluminous correspondence, magisterially edited by Myriam Chimènes (*Francis Poulenc, Correspondance, 1910-1963* (Fayard, 1994)); a valuable selection, beautifully translated by Sidney Buckland and accompanied by excellent notes, is available as *Francis Poulenc, 'Echo and Source'. Selected Correspondence 1915-1963* (Victor Gollancz, 1991). Parts of this book are as much about Cocteau as Poulenc, and I have drawn freely on Francis Steegmuller's superb *Cocteau. A Biography* (Macmillan, 1970). Translations are in general my own, except where lengthy extracts from letters translated by Buckland are cited.

On a personal note, I have, not for the first time, been able to draw on Beynon John's prodigious knowledge of French theatre and music, and also on Richard Griffiths's equally vast knowledge of French Catholicism. I am deeply indebted to Jon Croft of Absolute Press for taking up my proposals for a book on Poulenc, to Margaret Ralph who word-processed my manuscript, and to George Gandy who first encouraged me to listen carefully to Poulenc. My principal debt, however, is to Poulenc's niece, Madame Rosine Seringe, who generously provided a number of photographs from her personal collection and authorised my use of several other illustrations. It goes without saying that the views expressed in this study are solely my own.

R.D.E.B.
Lewes, East Sussex
November 2001

Legislation on homosexuality in France

Until the French Revolution, 'sodomy', whether homosexual or heterosexual, was considered a 'crime against nature' which, following canon law, could be punished by burning alive; seven so-called sodomites were so executed in Paris between 1714 and 1783. The post-revolutionary penal code of 1791 abolished the category of 'crimes against nature' and, since no other legislation was enacted, effectively decriminalised consensual homosexual acts *as such*. Homosexual acts were also not mentioned in the Napoleonic penal code of 1810, an omission often attributed, perhaps somewhat fancifully, to the fact that Napoleon's principal jurist, Jean-Jacques Cambacérès (1753-1824), was a well-known homosexual himself. However, homosexuals could be, and frequently were, charged for offences against public decency under Article 330 of the code, the general principle being that homosexual acts were not a crime in themselves, but could become so according to the circumstances in which they were practised. In effect, therefore, homosexual acts committed between consenting adult males in private were not subject to criminal procedure, 'adult' being defined (for both males and females) as eleven years old in 1810 and raised to 13 in 1863. Accordingly, there is no French equivalent of the trial of Oscar Wilde: they had the Dreyfus Affair instead. The law remained unchanged until 1942 when the Vichy regime raised the age of consent for heterosexual relations to 15, and to 21 for homosexual relations, a disparity retained by De Gaulle's first post-Liberation government and operative until 1974, when the age of homosexual consent was lowered to 18. In August 1982, the age of consent for both heterosexual and homosexual relations was set at 15. Needless to say, the Catholic Church's condemnation of *all* homosexual acts (but not, in theory, of homosexual 'orientation') remained unaltered by these changes in the civil code. (All the measures indicated refer to male homosexuality alone, female homosexuality never having been subject to legislation in France, though a ban of 1800 on 'cross-dressing', i.e. the wearing of trousers, was intermittently enforced in the early 1900s and under the Vichy regime, and female homosexuals could be, and occasionally were, charged under the same Article 330 as their male counterparts.)

'Homosexuel', 'pédéraste', 'inverti', etc.

The terms *'homosexuel'/'homosexualité'*, first attested in French in 1891, were not widely used in France until after the Second World War; in 1926, Poulenc's gay friend Max Jacob claimed mockingly that *'homosexuel'* meant *'homme au sexuel'*. The term most commonly used in Poulenc's life-time was *'pédéraste'*, more often used ecumenically to denote any male having sexual relations with, or desiring, other males (irrespective of age) than in the restrictive, and etymologically correct, sense of an adult male who has sex with, or desires, 'boys' (variously defined). An exception to this general rule is André Gide who, in his celebrated *Corydon* (1924), defends *'pédérastie'* in the restricted sense of the word, and is notably more reserved towards *'sodomie'* (his general term for sexual relations between *adult* men) and distinctly critical of *'invertis'* by which he designates men who assume the 'female role' in homosexual intercourse and desire to be (anally) possessed (see Alan Sheridan, *André Gide. A Life in the Present* (Penguin, 2000), pp. 376-8). The term *'uranien'/'uranisme'* is also widely used in medical, psychological and, occasionally, literary discourse, while, at the other end of the linguistic continuum, the commonest slang terms were (and are) *'tante'* and *'tapette'*, both with a strong connotation of effeminacy, and the more neutral *'pédé'*, *'pédale'*, *'pédoque'*, etc.); the expression *'en être'* (to be 'one of them') is also regularly used. The term 'gay', spelt and pronounced (approximately!) as in English, has become widely, and non-pejoratively, used since the 1980s.

Abbreviations

The following abbreviations are used:

A   Francis Poulenc, *A bâtons rompus. Ecrits radio-phoniques*,
          ed. Lucie Kayas (Actes Sud, 1999)

B   Sidney Buckland (ed.), *Francis Poulenc, 'Echo and Source'.*
          Selected Correspondence 1915-1963 (Victor Gollancz, 1991)

C   Myriam Chimènes (ed.), *Francis Poulenc.*
          Correspondance 1910-1963 (Fayard, 1994)

ECR   Francis Poulenc, *Entretiens avec Claude Rostand* (Julliard, 1954)

J   Francis Poulenc, *Journal de mes mélodies*, ed.
          Renaud Machart (Cicero Editeurs, 1993)

MFM   Francis Poulenc, *My Friends and Myself*,
          Conversations assembled by Stéphane Audel,
          trans. James Harding (Dennis Dobson, 1978)

Introduction

Francis Poulenc (1899-1963) was one of the most varied and accessible composers of the twentieth century. Extraordinarily precocious, he made his mark in the early 1920s as one of the loose association of young French composers known as Les Six, writing piano, chamber and ballet music notable for its wit, ebullience and insinuating lyricism. After 1929, the year of his first undoubted masterpiece, the *Concert champêtre* for harpsichord and orchestra, and of his highly personal ballet *Aubade*, Poulenc moved into writing musical settings, for single voice or chorus, of poems by some of the most adventurous French poets of the day – Guillaume Apollinaire (1880-1918), Max Jacob (1876-1944) and, above all, Paul Eluard (1895-1952) – and in 1935 formed a performing partnership with the great baritone Pierre Bernac (1899-1979) that was the French equivalent, in artistic if not in personal terms, of the Britten-Pears duumvirate in England. In August 1936, while visiting the shrine of the Black Virgin of Rocamadour in central France, Poulenc underwent a religious conversion which resulted, almost literally overnight, in the exquisite choral piece for female voices, *Litanies à la Vierge Noire*, the first of a whole series of specifically Catholic works that culminated in his bracing *Gloria* of 1959, perhaps the best known and most popular of all his compositions. During the German occupation of France, Poulenc set poems by leading resistance writers such as Eluard and Louis Aragon (1897-1982); and the post-war performance of the cantata *Figure humaine*, written in 1943 to texts by the former, established him retrospectively as *the* composer of the Resistance. Even as Paris was being liberated, Poulenc embarked on his first opera, *Les Mamelles de Tirésias*, based on the 1918 play of that name by Guillaume Apollinaire, which would be given its first performance in June 1947 with the soprano Denise Duval (born 1921), along with Bernac, Poulenc's other great performing partner, in the provocatively androgynous role of Thérèse-Tirésias. Between 1953 and 1956 Poulenc composed what is, by general consent, his greatest single work, the opera *Dialogues des Carmélites* (first performed at La Scala in January 1957), based on a text by the great French Catholic novelist Georges Bernanos (1888-1948) which dramatises the death by guillotine of 16 French Carmelite nuns at Compiègne in 1794. He brought his career to a triumphant artistic conclusion with the opera for single voice, *La Voix humaine* (1959), to a text by his old friend Jean Cocteau (1889-1963) and starring, once again, Denise Duval. He died suddenly of a heart attack in January 1963, by now widely regarded as the finest, and certainly as the most direct and enjoyable, French composer of the post Debussy/Ravel generation.

Despite his artistic and social success – from his early twenties Poulenc enjoyed access to the most exclusive Parisian salons and counted Picasso, Stravinsky and Colette as well as Britten and Bernstein and scores of other leading painters, writers and musicians amongst his personal friends – Poulenc was, as he put it towards the end of his life, an *'éternel inquiet'* (C p. 976), perpetually anxious about himself and his work, someone who, as he elsewhere says (C p. 326), had known much pleasure but little lasting happiness in his life. On at least three occasions – in 1928-30, in 1954-5 whilst composing the *Dialogues*, and again in 1958-9 – he suffered incapacitating breakdowns requiring treatment by drugs and, in one instance, hospitalisation, the crisis having been brought about in each case by a combination of artistic self-doubts and anguish over his personal relationships. Poulenc was essentially, but not exclusively, homosexual – his crisis of the late 1920s was caused by his rejection by a woman, Raymonde Linossier (1897-1930), whom he had known since childhood, followed almost immediately by her sudden death, and in 1946 he became the father of a daughter whom he never publicly acknowledged – and, as well as a number of more casual encounters and affairs, he enjoyed intense, and artistically crucial, sexual relationships with at least five men in the course of his life. Although Poulenc did not allow his Catholicism to stand in the way of his homosexuality, or his homosexuality in the way of his Catholicism, he undoubtedly suffered from the tension, if not the contradiction, between them, and much of his best music issues precisely from that tension and its always precarious resolution through art. Poulenc's music strikes many listeners as simple, even as simplistic, but the man who produced it was undoubtedly complex, even divided to the core of his being, and he knew that he had to assume that division, and the suffering it caused him, in order to create. 'At bottom,' he wrote in 1953, 'it may be that the worst of myself is the best of myself.' (C p. 776.)

In 1950, a close friend of Poulenc, the musicologist and broadcaster Claude Rostand, set the terms that have dominated critical discussion of his music to this day. There were, Rostand wrote in an article published in *Paris-Presse* in July that year, 'two people (*deux personnes*) in Poulenc: the monk (*le moine*) and the ragamuffin or street-urchin (*le voyou*)', the first responsible for the austere religious music from the *Litanies* onwards, and the second the 'naughty boy, sensual and seductive, mischievous and tender, graceful and brusque, aristocratic and popular', a child of the working-class *faubourgs* of Paris, who was responsible for the bulk of the secular music Poulenc had composed up to that time, above all his recently premiered first opera, *Les Mamelles de Tirésias*. Poulenc himself accepted this description of himself and his music, but rejected the implication that there was no connection – or that there was even an outright conflict – between his '*moine*' and '*voyou*' dimensions. No-one would ever believe, he wrote in 1939, that two pieces of music as different as the sprightly and cynical song 'Allons plus vite' to a text by Apollinaire and the grave and stately 'Vinea mea electa', the second of his *Quatre Motets pour un temps de pénitence*, could have been conceived and written *together* but this, he insisted, was precisely what had happened (C pp. 475-6). Exasperated by the continual invocation of Rostand's polarity, Poulenc came to insist more and more on being accepted and understood, both himself and his music, as a 'totality' and not as two warring 'halves' (C p. 916); 'Poulenc-Janus' he may be (J p. 34), but each of his 'faces' was as important as the other, distinct but interconnected 'persons' of a single human and artistic substance – himself.

The present study, likewise, both accepts and challenges the *moine/voyou* dichotomisation. It sees all of Poulenc's music as springing, ultimately, from a single, if scarcely simple, source and gives equal attention, and importance, to each of the supposed 'moieties' of his personality and work. Above all, it takes both his homosexuality and his Catholicism *seriously*, not seeking either to disguise or suppress the first or to view the latter as a derivative – or perhaps even a betrayal – of the former. Over and above its properly musical qualities, Poulenc's work points to a possible synthesis of sexuality and spirituality, of Eros (whether homosexual or heterosexual) and Agape, something that the institutional Church of which he became so devoted, if scarcely virtuous, an adherent has so conspicuously failed to realise even 40 years after this death.

The chapters that follow give a broadly chronological account of Poulenc's life and work, but aim at grounding both in their appropriate period and place, whence the opening chapter on the Parises – plural not singular, for, like the man himself, his native city was many, not one – of Francis Poulenc and also the third chapter, 'Homosexuality, Catholicism and modernism', which traces the links between modernism, Catholicism and homosexuality in inter-war France notably through the example of Jean Cocteau, texts by whom inspired both Poulenc's earliest work (*Cocardes* (1919)) and his last (*La Voix humaine* (1959) and *La Dame de Monte-Carlo* (1961)). A brief conclusion surveys the whole question of the place of homosexuality in Poulenc's life and work, and raises some questions regarding 'gay music' and 'gay musicology'.

The Parises of Francis Poulenc

Francis Poulenc was born in Paris on 7 January 1899 and died there on 30 January 1963. Although much, perhaps most, of his music was composed away from his native city, he was, first and last, a *musicien de Paris* whose work, even when inspired by other regions of France, as it increasingly was after his conversion to Catholicism in 1936, always had Paris as its ultimate reference point; 'the more I distance myself from Paris,' he said in a radio broadcast of 1949, 'the more I call on it to bear witness to my most intimate thoughts.' (A p. 103.) In the spring of 1927 Poulenc bought an imposing sixteenth-century country house named Le Grand Coteau on the outskirts of the village of Noizay in the Loire valley near Tours, no doubt with the intention of installing his childhood sweetheart, Raymonde Linossier, there as *châtelaine* and spouse. When she rejected his proposal and died shortly afterwards, Poulenc reluctantly took up residence in the house which, even after he was joined there by a local taxi-driver, Raymond Destouches (died 1988), continued to remind him of his early failure and loss. He never identified with either house or village, and certainly never drew inspiration from the delectable countryside around, though he did greatly relish the no less delectable Vouvray, the world-famous local white wine, that he purchased and consumed in abundance. For the rest of his life, Poulenc would, other commitments permitting, spend the spring, summer and early autumn at Noizay, devoting himself exclusively to composition and spending the winter attending concerts and socialising in Paris, the village's one virtue being that it was 'perfectly neutral' (J p. 49) and so allowed him to achieve total imaginative identification with the 'beloved places' that were his enduring inspiration: the Paris, Nogent-sur-Marne (see below) and Monte-Carlo of his youth, the Rocamadour of his religious conversion and similar sites in the Aveyron and Morvan which, as we shall see, he increasingly opposed to his Parisian origins. Cloistered in the 'prison' (C p. 562) or 'Carmel' (C p. 766) of Le Grand Coteau, Poulenc would recall, or fantasise

NOGENT-SUR-MARNE, WHICH LOOMED LARGE IN THE LIFE OF YOUNG POULENC

about, Paris 'with the heart of a lover' (J p. 21), particularly when, as in 1940 and again in 1944, the city was under threat of physical destruction. Significantly, it was at Noizay, between May and October 1944, that Poulenc wrote his most quintessentially 'Parisian' work, the hilarious gender-bending opera *Les Mamelles de Tirésias*, so fearful for the survival of his beloved Boulevard de La Chapelle or Grande Rue de Belleville that – or so he claimed more than once – whenever the words 'Paris' or 'the Seine' occur in Apollinaire's text, the accompanying music shifts in tone 'from buffoonery to gentle emotion' (A p. 197), thus creating 'oases of tenderness' (J p. 42) amidst the circum-ambient mayhem.

That the principal objects of Poulenc's concern were the utterly unfashionable Boulevard de La Chapelle and the Grande Rue de Belleville – the first a stretch of the *boulevards extérieurs* linking working-class (and now heavily 'black') Barbès-Rochechouart with the (then) communist stronghold around the Place de Stalingrad, the second the archetypal 'popular' street in the north-east of the city – is proof enough that the Paris of this wealthy country *propriétaire* was not, as one might expect, particularly after his conversion, the 'official' Paris of Notre-Dame, Sacré-Coeur or the Louvre, or even, for that matter, of that emblem of modernity and progress, the Eiffel Tower, which he, and four other young composers, had celebrated in the music to Cocteau's play *Les Mariés de la Tour Eiffel* (1921) that had made their names as the most exciting French musicians of the day. Poulenc was, it is true, born in the heart of the bourgeois city he now seemed to repudiate, in the staid and plush eighth *arrondissement*, at No. 2 Place des Saussaies, just to the north of the French President's official Parisian residence, the Palais de l'Elysée, and a few blocks due west of the most coldly classical church in the city, the Madeleine, much favoured by upper-class Catholics and a regular haunt, too, of Divine and 'her' lover Mignon in Jean Genet's *Notre-Dame-des-Fleurs* (1944, see the third chapter, 'Homosexuality, Catholicism and modernism'). Ironically, one of the streets leading into the Place des Saussaies is named after none other than Jean-Jacques Cambacérès, mentioned above, who is widely, if with some exaggeration, credited with the decriminalisation of homosexuality in France. Bisecting the street leading from Poulenc's birthplace to the church was the Rue d'Anjou where, in 1910, Cocteau and his mother took up residence at No. 10, while, debouching diagonally into the Place de la Madeleine from the east, was the Rue Duphot, the site chosen in 1920 or 1921 by one Louis Moÿsès for a bar called Le Gaya – not a name with the resonances it would have now – before moving a couple of streets to the west, to the Rue Boissy d'Anglas, and reopening as Le Boeuf sur le Toit after the title (itself derived from a Brazilian samba entitled 'O Boi No Telhado') of the celebrated 'Dadaist ballet' (with music by Darius Milhaud, text by Cocteau, and choreography by Massine), first performed at the Théâtre de la Comédie des Champs-Elysées in February 1920. No city lends itself more readily than Paris to topographical symbolism and here, within the space of a few hundred yards, were deployed the four cardinal points of Poulenc's imaginative universe: his upper-class origins (the Place des Saussaies) and the Church into which he would convert in his mid-thirties (La Madeleine, church of the Penitent Whore who wiped and worshipped her Lord's feet with her own loosened hair), with, standing athwart or across them, but also leading obliquely from one to the other, the worlds of homosexuality, art and wealthy Bohemianism (the Rues Cambacérès and d'Anjou) and the Boeuf sur le Toit into which Poulenc would be drawn from the age of 18 onwards. Did he but know it, the whole course of his life was mapped out in microcosm on the streets of the *quartier* in which he spent his childhood and early adolescence.

Poulenc's parents were Parisians by birth, though both came not from the bourgeois west of the city, but from the much poorer centre-east area known as the Marais, still in Poulenc's childhood the artisanal heartland of Paris, with its quintessentially *vieux Paris* mix of dilapidated sixteenth- and seventeenth-century *hôtels* and workshops in which dozens of *ébénistes*, *tapissiers* and *bronziers* still plied their trade; coincidentally, the Marais, and particularly the cafés, bars, restaurants and bookshops of the Rue Sainte-Croix-de-la-Bretonnière, is now the epicentre of gay social and cultural life in the capital. But, if the forebears of Poulenc's mother, Jenny Royer (1865-1915), had been Parisians since time immemorial, those of his father, Emile Poulenc (1855-1917), were recent immigrants from 'the Aveyron, that sturdy, mountainous area between the Auvergne and the Mediterranean basin', Poulenc indeed being 'a typical southern name' (MFM p. 56). Together with his brothers, Gaston Joseph and Camille, Emile Poulenc had founded the chemical company Poulenc Frères which, after the 1914-18 war, merged with Usines du Rhône to become the massive Rhône-Poulenc consortium that survives to this day, manufacturing chemical and pharmaceutical products as well as artificial textile fibres. Despite his very considerable wealth, Emile Poulenc remained a man of the Aveyron at heart and 'like the majority of Aveyronnais was deeply religious; he was, without any narrowness, quite magnificent in his faith (*magnifiquement croyant*)' (ECR p. 16), so much so that, in his later highly mythologised account of his complex inheritance, his son would claim that, 'When I pray, it is the Aveyronnais who reappears in me. The force of heredity. Faith is powerful amongst all the Poulencs.' (J p. 27.) Having thus assigned his *côté moine* to his meridional father, Poulenc, logically enough, ascribes his *côté voyou* to his 'ultra-Parisian' mother and her family. Jenny Poulenc was indeed largely indifferent to religion, and her tastes in music were correspondingly far removed from those of her husband. Whereas Emile Poulenc preferred Beethoven, Berlioz and César Franck to all other composers (though he could be moved to tears by Massenet's *Marie-Madeleine* as well as by *L'Enfance du Christ*), his wife delighted in what Poulenc calls '*la délicieuse mauvaise musique*' as well as in Mozart, Chopin, Schumann and Scarlatti, and it is to her, aided and abetted by her homosexual brother, Marcel Royer ('Uncle Papoum', 1862-1945), that Poulenc ascribes not only his love of high-spirited rhythms and sprightly melodies but also his early exposure to the most advanced music of his time; significantly, it was she, not her husband, who encouraged her son's precocious enthusiasm for Stravinsky (ECR pp. 19-21 and pp. 25-6).

Following the sudden deaths, within two years of each other, of both his mother and father, Poulenc moved in with his sister Jeanne (1887-1974) and her lawyer-husband André Manceaux (1883-1967), first at No. 76 Rue de Monceau (still in the eighth *arrondissement*) and then at No. 83 in the same street, where he occupied a bachelor flat above some former stables in the rear of the courtyard. Running alongside the ultra-bourgeois Parc de Monceau that is ringed by some of the largest and showiest mansions in Paris, Poulenc's new *quartier* was even more prim and precious than his self-styled '*ville natale*' around the Madeleine, and, not surprisingly, he loathed it. His hatred of the Plaine Monceau and, even more, the still more bourgeois suburb of Passy, further to the west, lasted throughout his life, and was as much musical as social (or sexual); in the last months of his life, he looked in vain for a boy soprano to take the solo part in his *Sept répons des ténèbres* whose voice would not be 'too "Plaine Monceau"' for music which, he insisted, required 'a pork butcher's or plumber's son from La Villette' in the north-east of the city if it was to be performed satisfactorily (C p. 1003). It was indeed towards the north, if not the north-east, of the city that Poulenc transferred his Parisian lodgings after he acquired the house at Noizay, when a friend offered him a *pied-à-terre* at his home at No. 24 Rue du Chevalier de la Barre in Montmartre, just behind the Basilica of Sacré-Coeur, where he regularly stayed until the mid-1930s. It was from here that he discovered the popular pleasures of the nearby Boulevard de La Chapelle (and probably, as we shall see, other pleasures as well), but the location was not without reverberations of a more spiritual order whose significance – and Poulenc, a regular consultant of all manner of cartomancers and palmists (see C pp 990 1), was nothing if not a reader of signs – would only be revealed many years later. Named after a 19-year-old aristocrat who had been tortured and executed at Abbeville in 1766 for having sung 'impious songs' and refused to doff his hat as a procession of Capucin monks passed by, the Rue du Chevalier de la Barre was for some years the home (at No. 40) of the ultra-Catholic novelist and essayist Léon Bloy (1846-1917) who, as we shall see, is the principal source of the idea of redemptive or vicarious suffering that is the theological mainspring of Georges Bernanos's *Dialogues des Carmélites* and, thus, of Poulenc's opera as well. It was to Bloy's home on the Rue du Chevalier de la Barre that, in June 1905, the young Jacques Maritain (1882-1973) and his Russian-Jewish wife, Raïssa (1883-1960), made their way at the start of the spiritual journey that would lead to their baptism and reception into the Roman Catholic Church a year later, whereafter, as the twin inspiration of the highly influential Meudon circle, they would be instrumental in bringing many intellectuals and artists – including, briefly and tumultuously, Jean Cocteau – into renewed communion with the Church (see the third chapter, 'Homosexuality, Catholicism and modernism'). On the other (western) side of the Butte Montmartre lay the Rue Ravignan where, at No. 7, Max Jacob, a friend of Poulenc since at least 1920, texts of whom he began to set to music in 1931, had, on 22 September 1909, had the vision of Jesus on the wall of his bedroom that would propel him, too, a homosexual and Jew, into the Church and ultimately into retreat, as a layman, at the Benedictine monastery of Saint-Benoît-sur-Loire near Orléans from which, in February 1944, he would be taken by the Gestapo to the concentration camp of Drancy in the north-eastern suburbs of Paris where he died of pneumonia the following month – a further link in the chain of sacrificial deaths which, as we shall see, had so decisive an influence on Poulenc's vision and work.

Poulenc spent most of his summer holidays as a child, adolescent and young man at his maternal grandparents' home at Nogent-sur-Marne just to the east of Paris beyond the Bois de Vincennes. Nogent is as important as Paris itself to Poulenc's life, self-image and music, and he often contrasts his 'Nogentais half-blood' with his 'Aveyronnais blood' (C p. 428), linking the first to his maternally derived 'naughty-boy side' (*'côté mauvais garçon'*, ECR pp. 17-18) and the *'délicieuse mauvaise musique'* that expressed it, and the second to the more spiritual and austere of his 'halves', along with its appropriate music, to the evident, and increasing, advantage of the latter. But Poulenc never sought to deny or suppress his 'Nogent side' and the 'Nogent work' (J p. 15) it created, and if the town remained both the source of his 'folklore' and his image of 'paradise' (ECR pp. 17-18), it was above all thanks to the numerous *guinguettes* and *bals musettes* that lined the northern banks of the Marne and the islands midstream, the Sunday afternoon Mecca of thousands of working-class Parisians from the east of the city, with its ubiquitous music and laughter commingling with the smell of cheap perfume and *pommes frites* to form a single intoxicating amalgam. It was here that, before, during and after the First World War, Poulenc absorbed the clarinet- and accordion-based music of the *bals musettes*, as played by such now forgotten popular virtuosi as Henri Christiné (1867-1941) and Vincent Scotto (1874-1952), many of them immigrants from the Poulencs' ancestral Auvergne who came over for the day from their Parisian bases around the Rue de Lappe (see below) in the east of the city. The music of Christiné and Scotto, that 'Rameau of the popular song', as Poulenc later described him (A p. 54), was not only freely transposed into the young composer's instrumental and vocal works of the 1920s, but still haunted him in the 1950s when he wrote the exquisite piano duet *L'Embarquement pour Cythère* (1951) and the Sonata for two pianos (1952-53) in memory of the now vanished Nogent of old. Both pieces were written for the American pianists Arthur Gold (1917-90) and Robert Fizdale (1920-95), known to him familiarly as 'les *kiddies*' or 'les *boys*', and *L'Embarquement* was accompanied by some characteristic, if highly unusual, interpretative advice: 'To get a really good hard-on, my naughty boys, don't play this dissolute idyll too fast.' (*'Pour que mes mauvais garçons bandent un bon coup, ne jouez pas trop vite cette crapuleuse idylle'*, C p. 985.) How better to indicate that if Nogent meant music, it also meant sex? How could it be otherwise when two of its midstream islands were known as the Ile de la Beauté and the Ile de l'Amour, to both of which the young Poulenc accompanied his still more precocious contemporary, the novelist and poet Raymond Radiguet (1903-23), native of the nearby town of Saint-Maur, future lover of Cocteau (and possibly of Jacob as well), whose early and terrible death from typhoid in December 1923 would, as we shall see, drive Cocteau to seek double consolation in opium and the Church. Poulenc never forgot his idyllic afternoons and evenings in the company of the author of *Le Diable au corps* (1923) – how he would love to have written the music for the 1946 film of the novel (J p. 53) – and belatedly he set Radiguet's poem 'Paul et Virginie' to music that year, as well as dedicating to his memory settings of two poems by Apollinaire (1880-1918), dead at 38 from a combination of Asian flu and the after-effects of head wounds received in the trenches. Apollinaire, Radiguet, Jacob: the association between sex, art, suffering and death became ever more fixed in Poulenc's mind and his music.

There is, finally, what we might call *le troisième Paris*, neither east nor west, right bank or left bank, but present in shadows and corners throughout the city: the Paris of *le troisième sexe*, not the effulgent 'Gay Paree' of legend but 'Paris gay', its barely visible underside and antithesis.[1] *Le troisième Paris* was not a *quartier*, or even a *quartier* within a *quartier*, but was to be found virtually everywhere in the interstices of the city, rather than on its margins, just below, beside or behind the brightly lit boulevards of the straight majority. The topography of 'queer Paris' was as nuanced and differentiated as, according to Gide, homosexuality was itself. Those who, like Gide, the novelist and dramatist Henry de Montherlant (1895-1972) and the novelist Roger Peyrefitte (1907-2000), were pederasts in the strict sense of the word headed towards the so-called *kermesses*, or amusement arcades, located actually *on* the *grands boulevards*, and, above all, to the Kermesse Berlitz on the Boulevard des Capucines between the Madeleine and the Opéra or the Kermesse Clichy on the boulevard of that name which marks the southern limit of Montmartre, at both of which adolescent boys could be picked up with considerable ease and relative security, or haunted – in the case of Montherlant and Peyrefitte, the 'Castor and Pollux' of Parisian pederasty, often operating in tandem, the word does not seem overloaded – any number of cheap cinemas, known as *bibliothèques* (libraries) in the trade, in the reasonable hope of finding *un roman* (a novel, a romance) or, failing that, *un bouquin* (variously a book, a young buck or the mouthpiece of a pipe – '*faire une pipe*' being the standard slang for fellatio). Others made their way, according to taste and means, to one or another of the many gay cafés and bars in Montparnasse and Montmartre, a few of them relatively chic, but most, like La Chaumière on the Rue Gabrielle below Sacré-Coeur, more a matter of 'wooden tables, a moth-eaten carpet, the hint of a tablecloth and a lot of dust' or, like Graff's on the Place Blanche just by the Moulin Rouge, a 'regular', if rowdy, tavern-cum-restaurant till nine in the evening, after which, as the cinemas and theatres emptied, 'a tumultuous throng of boys invaded it, shrieking like old ladies'(André Du Dognon, *Les Amours bussonnières* (1948)).

Between the two wars, there were a number of dance halls at which homosexuals could consort more or less openly, especially the *bals musette* on the Rue de Lappe in the east of the city close to the present Opéra de la Bastille, an Auvergnat enclave so popular with Parisian gays that one wit, 'Willy', the one-time husband of Colette, proposed in 1927 that its name be changed to Rue de Loppe (Fag Street). The famous mid-Lent ball at the Magic City, on the Rue Cognacq-Jay midway between the Eiffel Tower and the Assembleé Nationale, attracted homosexuals from across Europe until it was closed down, for reasons that remain obscure, following the fascist riots in Paris in February 1934 (see the fourth chapter, 'Black Virgin: Poulenc at Rocamadour'); the Bal de la Montagne Sainte-Geneviève in the Quartier

Latin was also a much favoured locale, especially for transvestites. Public baths, Turkish baths and gymnasiums also had their *habitués*, as did the swimming pool of the Union chrétienne des jeunes gens (the French YMCA) on the Rue de Trévise, a couple of blocks from the Folies-Bergère. 'Open air' pick-ups could be easily made on the Champs-Elyseés, in the Jardin des Tuileries where the statue of a wild boar had been a gay landmark since the 1830s, at the Trocadéro in the west of the city, and on the Champ de Mars on the left bank opposite, along the criss-crossing avenues and paths around the Eiffel Tower. Finally, and most dangerously, since around them lurked both muggers and police, were the now vanished wrought-iron *vespasiennes* (public urinals), known to homosexuals as *théières* (teapots) or *tasses*, some of which, like those on the Place de Clichy and the Place de la Bourse by the Paris Stock Exchange, attained legendary status in the inter-war annals of *le troisième Paris*. *La tasse* was the shrine of a whole sexual counter-cult, with its priests, acolytes and constantly changing congregation; when the Word became Flesh, said Genet, it also became *Tasse*.[2]

The Paris of the 1920s and 1930s was, in short, honeycombed with concealed but accessible gay spaces, and every *quartier*, be it in the patrician west or the plebeian east, offered both opportunity and threat, not least the area around the Madeleine which, several times, is cited as the 'headquarters of debauchery', the *temple noir* where every sect and denomination could find satisfaction.[3] Poulenc obviously knew of the existence of le *troisième Paris*: how far did he make use of the possibilities it offered? Here we have only fragments of what may or may not be 'evidence', like the aside in *Journal de mes mélodies* (p. 25) where Poulenc says that 'I have hung around the streets of Paris so much at night (*J'ai tant traîné la nuit dans Paris*) that, more than any other musician, I know the rhythm of a slipper (*une pantoufle*) as it glides over asphalt on a May evening', a curious detail made even curiouser when Peyrefitte tells us that Montherlant prized what he called '*le pantouflard*' above all other conquests, namely 'the son of a *concierge* or the like, hanging around in slippers in the vicinity of the caretaker's lodge or his father's workshop'.[4] Then there is a letter from Poulenc's fellow composer (and fellow homosexual) Henri Sauguet (1901-89) sent from Toulouse in August 1936, just a few days before Poulenc's 'conversion' at Rocamadour. Between 1930

and 1933, at a time when Poulenc regularly stayed at a friend's on the nearby
Rue du Chevalier de la Barre (see above), Sauguet had lived, along with Max
Jacob (then on a ten-year sabbatical-in-reverse from Saint-Benoît-sur-Loire)
and Maurice Sachs (1906-44), of whom much more anon, at the Hôtel
Nollet on the street of that name which, hardly fortuitously, led directly into
the gay Mecca – Peyrefitte called its *kermesse* 'la kaaba' – of the Place and
Boulevard de Clichy. By 1936, Sauguet was living on the outskirts of
Toulouse and wrote to Poulenc bewailing the demolition of the local
vespasiennes, those 'furtive temples where the manual intrigues that we know
are set up and resolved (*où se nouent et se dénouent les intrigues manuelles que nous
connaissons*, C p. 418): presumably his correspondent was no stranger to the
plaisirs de la tasse. One may assume that Poulenc knew the *bals musette* on the
Rue de Lappe and elsewhere, but if he visited Graff's, the Taverne Liégeoise,
Chez ma cousine, Le Maurice-Bar, Le Palmyrium, or any other gay cabaret
or bar in Montmartre, or frequented the Turkish baths on the Rue
Tiquetonne or the Rue de Ternes, or the swimming pool on the Rue de
Pontoise in the Quartier Latin, or any of the hundred and one gay locales
mentioned in the literature, he says nothing of it in his published
correspondence.

In 1936, shortly before his 'conversion', Poulenc acquired a permanent *pied-
à-terre* in Paris, moving into a *chambre de bonne* in the *immeuble* in which his
Uncle Papoum had his apartment, at No. 5 Rue de Médicis, overlooking the
Jardin du Luxembourg, a suitably neutral location for one whose life was
becoming increasingly peripatetic as his growing fame (and continuing need
to perform) led to one musical engagement after another. When Uncle
Papoum died in 1945, Poulenc moved down into an apartment adjoining that
which his flamboyant relative had just 'vacated', and it was here that Poulenc
himself would die in January 1963. A commemorative plaque marks the
immeuble, and a nearby square has been renamed in his honour, though
connoisseurs of toponymic ironies may note that the street on which Poulenc
would spend all his post-conversion visits to Paris leads from the Rue Gay-
Lussac to a square named after the notoriously homophobic Catholic
diplomat-poet Paul Claudel....

The Ox on the Roof:
Poulenc, Les Six and the 1920s

'I did not go to Oxford or Cambridge,' wrote the Irish novelist George Moore in his *Confessions of a Young Man* (1888), 'I went to the Café Nouvelle Athènes.'[5] For almost a century, from, say, 1860 to 1950, the café was, in its various forms, the pivotal institution of Parisian artistic and intellectual life, far more so than the salon, to say nothing of the university *amphithéâtre* or seminar room which took over from both in the course of the 1960s. For the impressionists, it was first the Café Guerbois on the present Avenue de Clichy in the north-west of the city and then the Nouvelle Athènes on the Place Pigalle at the entrance to Montmartre, while their decadent and early modernist successors foregathered, argued and drank at the Lapin Agile at the summit of the Butte or at the Chat Noir at its base. Around 1910, the centre of gravity shifted, with Picasso, from the cafés of Montmartre in the north to those of Montparnasse in the south, to which, after the war, the Dadaists riposted by establishing their headquarters midway between north and south, at the Café Certa in the now demolished Passage de l'Opéra; when, in their turn, Breton and Aragon broke with Dada, they led their followers back north to the Café Cyrano on the Place Blanche and north-east to the Batifol on the Rue du Faubourg-Saint-Martin which, between them, became the joint permanent secretariat of the nascent surrealist movement. As artistic and intellectual life polarised after the armistice, one of the few points of intersection and exchange between the contending movements and groups was Le Gaya, located, symbolically, on neutral terrain in the wealthy hub of the city, in what Poulenc always called his *'ville natale'*: the streets that led in and out of the Place de la Madeleine.[6] Le Gaya, as we have seen, was founded by Louis Moÿsès, an enterprising young man whose one claim to fame, such as it was, was that he came from Charleville, Rimbaud's home town, and that, as a boy, he had lived in a house once occupied by the author of *Une saison en enfer*. Not so much a café as a nightclub-cum-bar, Le Gaya had white-tiled walls that reminded some *habitués* of a metro station or up-market *pissoir*, its other decorative feature being a huge picture of an eye entitled *L'Oeil cacolydate* by one of its regulars, the immensely wealthy Dadaist painter-poet Francis Picabia (1879-1953), that hung over the bar and around which eminences of *beau monde* and *demi-monde* were invited to inscribe their names along with whatever came into their heads: *'couronne de mélancolie'* (crown of melancholy) wrote Cocteau, presumably not unaware that *'couronne'* meant 'anus' in the gay argot of the time.[7] So many celebrities from *le Tout-Paris* and what an earlier age would have called *la Bohème* were drawn to the *boîte* (club) that, some time in late 1921 or early 1922, Moÿsès decided to move to larger premises on the nearby Rue Boissy d'Anglas and, as we have seen, gave the new locale the inspired name of Le Boeuf sur le Toit. A unique chapter in the social and artistic history of Paris was about to begin.

If, in one *habitué*'s words, Le Boeuf was 'the crossroad of destinies, the cradle of loves, the matrix of disputes, the navel of Paris',[8] the navel's navel, so to speak, was inevitably Cocteau, and to enumerate only the best known of those who came under his, and its, spell is to begin to appreciate the extraordinary criss-crossing and overlapping in the Parisian society of the time. Out of the pages of the Almanach de Gotha stepped the Comte and Comtesse Etienne de Beaumont, the 'originals' of the count and countess in Radiguet's posthumous novel *Le Bal du comte d'Orgel* (1924); the Prince and Princess Edmond de Polignac, he a homosexual, she, the American-born Winnaretta Singer of sewing-machine fame, the lesbian lover of, amongst others, the American painter Romaine Brooks, the English composer Ethel Smyth and the thoroughly cosmopolitan Violet Trefusis; the Comte Jean de Polignac, nephew of the Prince, and his wife Marie-Blanche, two of Poulenc's very closest friends at whose château de Kerbastic in Britanny, known as 'Keker', he frequently stayed; and, last but very much not least, the Vicomte and Vicomtesse (Marie-Laure) de Noailles, the most adventurous and influential art patrons of the time, who commissioned both Buñuel and Dali's surrealist extravaganza *L'Age d'or* (1930) and Cocteau's first, and pathbreaking, film *Le Sang d'un poète* (1932) and who, in what is widely regarded as the swansong both of Les Six and of the whole world of Le Boeuf, would stage Poulenc's highly personal ballet *Aubade* at a private party held in June 1929 at their sumptuous town house on the Place des Etats-Unis in the ultra-chic sixteenth *arrondissement* (see below). From the world of industry came André Citroën, from fashion Coco Chanel, from ballet the two Serges, Diaghilev and Lifar, while the singers Mistinguett and Maurice Chevalier headed the stars of popular stage and screen. To the many painters and poets who were, or would become, close friends of Poulenc – Picasso, Jacob, Marie Laurencin, Jacques-Emile Blanche, Valentine and Jean Hugo (great-grandson of Victor) – must be added whole galaxies of modernist luminaries: the poets Léon-Paul Fargue, Blaise Cendrars and Pierre Reverdy, the painters Fernand Léger and André Derain, the Roumanian-born sculptor Brancusi. Despite their loathing of Cocteau, Breton and Aragon made frequent forays into the territory he held as his own, while from over the channel came the aristocrat-composer Lord (Gerald) Berners (1883-1950), perhaps the nearest English equivalent to the early Poulenc, and the painter Christopher Wood, a close friend of both Cocteau and Jacob, who, in 1930, would commit suicide by throwing himself in front of a train on Salisbury station. Finally, when in Paris, the Prince of Wales, the future Edward VIII and Duke of Windsor, was a regular visitor, bringing whole droves of Binkies and Bunties in his wake.

All these, and many, many more, talked and drank night after night – it was the age of 'cocktails et *re*cocktails', in Poulenc's words (C p. 105), as well as of other Anglicisms, 'le *bridge*' (of which Poulenc was an avid and expert player), 'la *surprise-party*' and 'le *nervous breakdown*' – and, above all, foxtrotted, Charlestoned and tangoed to 'Dardanella', 'Ain't She Sweet?', 'Breezin' Along with the Breeze' and 'Japanese Sandman', as performed by, amongst others, the composer-pianist Jean Wiéner, a close friend of Poulenc who also organised concerts at which Poulenc's music was regularly played, and a black American banjo player and saxophonist named Vance Lowry, who, said Darius Milhaud, one of the five composers of Les Six who regularly attended, were capable of shifting, virtually without transition, 'from fashionable ragtime and foxtrots to the most celebrated works of Bach'.[9] Amongst the nightly whirl at Le Boeuf, two sub-groups, themselves overlapping at significant points, are particularly relevant to the present enquiry. First, the *boîte*'s clientele included a sizeable number of current or future Catholics, not just nominal Catholics by family and baptism, but committed – either now, later, or for a time – practisers of their faith: Paul Claudel, an improbable nightclubber, perhaps, but a frequent visitor when on leave from ambassadorial duties abroad; the painter and stage decorator; Jean Hugo, who would be baptised in 1931 with Maritain as godfather; and the poet Pierre Reverdy, another member of the Maritain circle, who would shortly follow Max Jacob's example and withdraw, with his wife, to the precincts of the great Benedictine monastery of Solesmes in the Sarthe, famous, then and now, for the beauty of its Gregorian chant. Closer still to Poulenc, his exact contemporary and fellow member of Les Six, Georges Auric (1899-1983), called regularly, while still in his teens, on Léon Bloy during the last two years of the prophet-novelist's life, his visits often coinciding with those of the Maritains. Secondly, in Jean Hugo's words, 'Greek love [*sic*] was no stranger to the natives' of Le Boeuf, and amongst those *habitués* known to *'faire la promenade'*, in the private language of the *boîte*,[10] were Prince Edmond de Polignac (he and his lesbian wife having an 'arrangement' of obvious mutual convenience), André Gide (escaping, as so often, from his cousin-wife Madeleine), Diaghilev and Lifar, Marshall Lyautey, the architect of French colonialism in Morocco and a well-known, even ostentatious, homosexual, and, amongst the visitors from abroad, Gerald Berners, Kit Wood and ... Edward, Prince of Wales, who many Parisian gays of that time, and later, claim – nay, *know* – to have been queer.[11] Thirdly, and most interestingly from our point of view, is the significant number of *habitués* who were both homosexuals and present, or future, Roman Catholics: Cocteau and at least two of his lovers, Jean Desbordes and Jean Bourgoint (see the third chapter, 'Homosexuality, Catholicism and modernism'), Max Jacob, the novelists Julien Green and Marcel Jouhandeau (1888-1975) – the latter the anonymous author of *Tirésias* (1954), as lyrical a paean to the joys of being anally penetrated as can ever have been written – as well as Poulenc himself, and the extraordinary Maurice Sachs whose unique spiritual, sexual and political trajectory will exercise us greatly in the chapter that follows. Not for nothing did Sachs later write that, in the early and mid-1920s, 'the jargon (*vocabulaire*) of Le Boeuf sur le Toit was spoken amongst the friends of God (*les amis de*

Dieu), and the language of monasteries at Le Boeuf sur le Toit.' It was typical of both the age and the individual that when, after his 'conversion' in 1925, a friend learned that Sachs 'was going to *le Séminaire*', the friend immediately assumed that this must be some fashionable *boîte de nuit* that had recently opened.[12]

If Moÿsès had chosen Le Boeuf sur le Toit as the eye- and ear-catching name for his *boîte*, it was in recognition of the fact that it was the new music, rather than the, now, not so new painting, that most perfectly captured the frenetic and almost wilfully superficial spirit of the new decade. Les Six owed not just their name but their very existence to two articles by the music critic, Henri Collet (1885-1951), published in the journal *Comoedia* in January 1920 that singled them out, rather arbitrarily, as exemplars of a new, and quintessentially French, musical style. The revolution of which their music was, in reality, an edulcorated and domesticated derivative had been jointly precipitated some years before by Stravinsky's *Rite of Spring*, an early performance of which Poulenc had attended as a 14-year-old at the Théâtre des Champs-Elysées, and by Erik Satie's dizzyingly audacious ballet *Parade* premiered by the Ballets russes (text by Cocteau, costumes and *décor* by Picasso, choreography by Massine, conducted by Ansermet: talent was not exactly thin on the ground) at the Théâtre du Châtelet on 18 May 1917. Like practically every other Parisian artist of the day, Poulenc, by now a highly impressionable 18-year-old, was present at the celebratedly raucous first performance, following which he became a close friend of Satie until they fell out in 1924. An occasional visitor to Le Boeuf, Satie (1866-1925) was also a peripheral member of the Maritain circle who, having previously been the one adept of his own Universal Church of Jesus Christ the Conductor, returned to the rather larger Holy Roman Catholic Church on his deathbed – 'because', or so he allegedly said, 'it gives them pleasure' (*'puisque ça leur fait plaisir'*), 'them' being, inevitably, those ever-vigilant soul-savers, the Maritains – though, if he had any sex life, he kept it as hermetically private as his famously impenetrable one-room lodgings at Arcueil.[13]

Cocteau followed up the *succès de scandale* of *Parade* by publishing a sequence of aphorisms entitled *Le Coq et l'arlequin* in the spring of 1918, which has come to be seen as Les Six's manifesto even before Les Six officially existed; Poulenc, however, insisted that Cocteau was merely the group's impressario, not its inspiration (ECR p. 45). 'I demand a truly French music of France', Cocteau famously declared, denouncing the baleful influence of Wagner and 'Wagnerism' on contemporary French music which, in his view, had drowned the sharp outlines of authentic French classicism beneath a miasma of Teutonic opacity, producing the monster of musical 'impressionism', be it 'Franckism' or 'Debussyism', that it was Satie's (and his own) mission to destroy. Henceforth, anything 'nebulous, deliquescent or superfluous' was to be purged in the name of clarity of structure, purity of sound and simplicity of emotion. Music, like painting, should take its inspiration from the everyday, the modern, the urban – from street fairs and circuses, from music hall and *café-concert* and, not least, from the jazz which, with the arrival of American troops in France, was beginning to sweep through the *boîtes* and *salons* of Paris.[14] 'I want there to be music built that I can inhabit like a house', Cocteau concluded, echoing Satie's celebrated concept of 'furniture music' (*'musique d'ameublement'*), a music of the quotidian, not of the 'eternal', of the real, not of the mystical or mythical, in short, what, in a remarkable insight in a letter of May 1920, Poulenc would call 'horizontal' as opposed to 'perpendicular' music (C p. 107). If all this seemed far ahead of what the concert-going public could take, so much the better, since, Cocteau averred, using capital letters so that his point would not be lost, 'WHEN A WORK OF ART SEEMS IN ADVANCE OF ITS TIME, IT IS SIMPLY BECAUSE ITS TIME HAS YET TO CATCH UP WITH IT.'[15]

By 1917, Poulenc was already writing, unaided and uncluttered by any manifesto or programme, music that met Cocteau's demand for 'a return to simplicity' and to 'the poetry of childhood', music that was 'straightforward, clear, luminous'. That he had received no formal compositional training was, at this stage of his career, to his undoubted advantage. Having learned at his mother's side the basics of the piano, he was passed on for further instruction to the Catalan pianist, Ricardo Viñes (1875-1943), who was yet another acolyte of Bloy and a future member of the Maritain circle. At the same time, his friendship with Raymonde Linossier gained him admittance, while still in his teens, to one of the shrines of Parisian modernism, the *Maison des Amis du*

Livre, the international bookshop, founded and owned by Adrienne Monnier (1892-1955) and frequented by Joyce, Pound and other expatriate writers, on the Rue de l'Odéon in the Quartier Latin. A regular attender of the bookshop's poetry readings, Poulenc thus gained early access to a further network of artists and writers, many of whose lives and works would intermesh with his own: Apollinaire, Aragon, Breton, Valéry, Claudel, Larbaud, Soupault, Desnos and – most crucial of all, though it would be 20 years before its potential was realised – Paul Eluard. On 11 December 1917, still four weeks short of his eighteenth birthday, Poulenc became an overnight sensation with the performance, at the Théâtre du Vieux-Colombier on the street of the same name, also in the Quartier Latin, of his first published work, the voguishly entitled *Rapsodie nègre*. Dedicated to Satie and scored for piano, string quartet, flute, clarinet and baritone voice, the *Rapsodie* sets the tone and structure for a very substantial portion of Poulenc's pre-1936 output. Switching continually between graceful lyricism and maniacal high spirits, its five brief movements pivot on a mock-melancholy intermezzo entitled 'Honouloulou' that sets to music a 'poem' by one 'Makoko Kangourou', the alleged 'Liberian' author of a literary spoof designed to satirise the current Parisian craze for Africana, bogus and genuine. At the last moment, the scheduled singer took fright and refused to take part in the musical mayhem, leaving Poulenc, who, having just been called up, was in military uniform, with no choice but to stand up and intone the pseudo-griot's plangent refrain:

> *Honouloulou, poti lama!*
> *Honouloulou, Honouloulou,*
> *Kati moko, mosi bolou*
> *Ratakou sira, polama!*

It was the kind of stunt that accorded perfectly with the febrile mood of the times, and reputedly prompted Ravel, who was in the audience, to declare – though whether in admiration or sarcasm is unclear – that 'what's good about Poulenc is that he invents his own folklore',[16] perhaps the most perceptive comment ever made about the composer.

Despite military service (spent mainly in the vicinity of Paris and always well away from the front), Poulenc's reputation 'rose without trace' with each new composition – the well-known *Mouvements perpétuels* for piano (1918), *Le Bestiaire* (1919) to words by Apollinaire, *Cocardes* (also 1919) to poems by Cocteau – and he was instantly promoted to the front rank of the musical avant-garde, variously and successively dubbed *'les sportifs de la musique'*, *'les nouveaux jeunes'* and, most enduringly, 'les Six'. Les Six were not a concerted 'movement' or 'group' in the manner of Dada or Surrrealism, but a loose association of like-minded friends who, for a time, found that it suited their careers to be publicly linked one with the other. As such, it was never founded or dissolved, though its members went their own way after 1924 (when Jean Wiéner, the pianist at Le Boeuf, suspended his concerts), and its final demise is often symbolically linked with the Wall Street Crash of October 1929 which, in Maurice Sachs's words, abruptly brought the 'Ox down from the Roof'.[17] More or less conterminous, therefore, with the 1920s, Les Six brought together two Catholics, one practising, one lapsed (Auric and Poulenc), one Provençal Jew (the hugely prolific Darius Milhaud (1892-1974), a former personal secretary to Claudel in Brazil and composer of music for several of his plays), one French-born Protestant of Swiss extraction and nationality (Arthur Honegger (1892-1955), also a future collaborator with Claudel, and whose orchestral suites *Pacific 231* (1923) and *Rugby* (1928) are the fullest realisations of the group's quest for modernity), one woman whose early brilliance was partially stifled by two unhappy marriages and persistent financial problems (Germain Tailleferre (1892-1983)) and one future communist (Louis Durey (1888-1979)) who would later set to music texts by Mao Tse-tung and Ho Chi Minh and compose forgotten agitprop pieces such as *Quatre chants de lutte pour l'unité de la jeunesse républicaine* for a variety of left-wing causes. Brought together by a journalist's tag, Les Six ultimately had little in common beyond their shared opposition to 'Wagnerism' and 'Debussyism' (but not to Debussy himself, as Poulenc quickly stressed), their preference for terse, uncluttered musical forms and their desire to incorporate into their work the rhythms, melodies and sharply contrasting moods of the music of the popular *faubourgs* and *lieux de plaisance* that Poulenc knew so well. Theirs was a Dadaism minus the demonic and without the despair, a mixture of exuberance and impertinence all too readily acceptable to the aesthetes and socialites of Le Boeuf sur le Toit. Anxious, like their public, to repress every memory of the horrors Europe had so recently been through (but which they, Durey apart, had been able to avoid), they wrote 'horizontal' music that was largely content, wittily and elegantly, to espouse the surface of things, and eschewed both the possible heights above and the undoubted depths below in favour of an all too facile popularity. Only Poulenc and Honegger achieved real greatness as composers, and then only by transcending the prescriptions of *Le Coq et l'arlequin* which, if they liberated in one sense, severely restricted in another.

The group (minus Durey, who may already have seen through their empty rebelliousness) collaborated on the Pythonesque ballet *Les Mariés de la Tour Eiffel* (1921, text by Cocteau), which Poulenc followed up with a succession of chamber pieces characterised by their juxtaposition of ingratiating lyricism and boisterous 'leg-Poulenc' – the composer soon gained a following in chic musical circles in London – and one substantial orchestral work, the ballet *Les Biches* (choreography by Nijinska, costumes and *décor* by Marie Laurencin), the circumstances of whose first performance in Monte-Carlo in January 1924 will be described in the chapter that follows. Based on an 'argument' by Poulenc himself and 'born of the near-mythical *"beau monde"*, for the delectation of Beautiful People', *Les Biches* has been well described as domesticated Stravinsky, 'a Frenchified *Les Noces*'[18] which is of interest, musically, for its stylish eclecticism and, psychologically and culturally, for its occasional hints at sexual inversion beneath the ballet's overt subject of country-house courtship and marriage. It established Poulenc as the *nec plus ultra* of modish sophistication – '*les riches* love les *Biches*', said Marie Laurencin, more or less[19] – and pointed the way to his brilliant *Concert champêtre* (1929) for harpsichord and orchestra, written for Wanda Landowska, an early example of what would now be called polystylism in which the whole of French music from the Middle Ages to the present, via the classical and the baroque, is scintillatingly convoked to create a never-never-land that is not so much rural as suburban: a mixture of Nogent-sur-Marne and the Ermenonville of Rousseau blended with Landowska's estate at Saint-Leu-la-Forêt to the north of Paris where parts of it were written, with, for the first time, just a hint of the 'deserts of vast eternity' stretching beyond.[20]

By the end of 1917, with the *Concert champêtre* well under way, Poulenc might well look back with satisfaction on what he had achieved. Still under 30, he was the musical darling of *le Tout-Paris*, his works had been acclaimed by some of the greatest composers of the day (Ravel, Stravinsky), he was, or appeared to be, financially secure, having inherited a substantial fortune from his father, and he had just purchased an imposing country mansion with the express purpose of installing his childhood sweetheart, Raymonde Linossier, there as his wife.[19] Then, suddenly, within the space of six months, everything unravelled and, by the middle of 1928, he was desperately unhappy both personally and artistically, in each case for reasons connected with the unresolved question of his sexual identity. In the first instance, it became clear to Poulenc that Raymonde did not reciprocate his undeclared *amor de lonh* which, if nothing else, enabled him to evade the issue of his repressed homosexuality. A forthright, cultivated and ambitious young woman, already a qualified lawyer and respected Orientalist, with an important position at the Musée Guimet, Raymonde probably suspected Poulenc's underlying sexual orientation, and it may be significant that, in the only letter from her to the composer that survives, she reveals herself to be decidedly unsympathetic towards the 'chic, idle, homosexual element' (*'l'élément chic, inoccupé et pédéraste'*) that foregathered for Satie's funeral in July 1925 at Arcueil (see C p. 256). Crippled with anguish, Poulenc was reduced, in July 1928, to begging Raymonde's elder sister, Alice, in effect to propose to her on his behalf; if she did so, the proposal was evidently rejected, leaving Poulenc to pour his disarray into the ballet *Aubade* that the de Noailles had recently commissioned from him for performance the following year.

In his misery, Poulenc began, as he so often would, to identify with the sufferings of others: with Henri Sauguet whose partner Christian Hardouin died in August 1928 (see C p. 292) and then with the mezzo-soprano Claire Croiza (1882-1946) whose 'painful calvary' (*'douloureux calvaire'*, C p. 308) – she had been deserted by Honegger, the father of her child – reminded him of his own, a first, and significant, instance of Poulenc's identifying himself both with the anguish of a woman abandoned and, if only metaphorically, with the Passion of Christ. Then, some time in early 1929, he embarked upon what was almost certainly his first passionate homosexual relationship, with the painter and gallery owner Richard Chanlaire, with whom he enjoyed an unfettered openness that could not be further from his timidity with Raymonde whom he did not even have the courage to address as *'tu'* (C p. 795):

> You (*tu*) have changed my life, you are the sun of my thirty years, a reason for living and working. Throughout long months of solitude I called to you without knowing you. Thank you for having at last come. [...] Work too, Richard, work to make me happy. My beloved friend, I huddle in your arms, my head against your heart; keep me there for a long, long, long time (*longtemps, longtemps, longtemps*), so that death alone can snatch me from so soft a cradle.

> Letter of 10 May 1929, C p. 304

Ten days after sending this letter to Chanlaire, he confided his 'great, grave secret' (*'mon gros secret, mon grave secret'*) to Valentine Hugo, confessing his pain at having to conceal his 'anomaly' (his word) but making it clear that nothing now counted for him apart from the 'agonising *amour fou*' he felt for Chanlaire (C p. 304). Such tensions and longings might have produced music of searing intensity, had Poulenc been able and willing to confront them. As it is, at least insofar as his output of the 1920s is concerned, one readily assents to the view expressed by one critic (Andrew Clements of *The Guardian*) during Poulenc's centenary year (1999) that 'no twentieth-century composer worked harder or more consistently at covering his emotional tracks': 'When confronted with potential profundity, Poulenc shied away, stayed on the surface, sheltered beneath that insistently charming persona.' It is certainly true that his music of the 1920s (and, in the same critic's view, of his entire musical output) 'seemed daring but was really utterly safe', its lyricism too slick and seductive, its high-spiritedness either merely jokey or manic, its predictable alternations between the two moods almost designed to exclude the possibility of anything of greater musical and emotional substance transcending the two. To the question 'Did the real Poulenc ever come out?'[21] there is – once more as far as his music of the 1920s is concerned – only the partial response of the ballet *Aubade* (1929) whose very title bespeaks an effort to emerge from night into day, from emotional confusion to maturity, and to which, as Poulenc's most personal musical utterance prior to the mid-1930s, we must devote rather more attention than to the works considered so far.

In conversation with Claude Rostand in 1954, Poulenc described *Aubade* as 'an amphibious work' (ECR p. 80), and so indeed it is, not only musically, but also emotionally and sexually. It had, as we have seen, been commissioned by Charles and Marie-Laure de Noailles for private performance at a *soirée* to be held at their Parisian residence in June 1929. Begun in a 'state of joy', in Poulenc's description, it rapidly floundered under the weight of his emotional misery throughout 1928, and in February 1929 he wrote to Charles de Noailles, telling him that he felt unable to complete the work even 'in tears' and asked to be relieved of the commission on the grounds that 'life has broken me to such a point that I no longer know who I am' (C p. 299). Then, presumably under the influence of his love for Chanlaire, he was able to resume the work later in the spring and eventually wrote it quickly between May and June 1929, partly in Paris and partly on the de Noailles' country estate near Fontainebleau, appropriately enough for a 'Janus-faced composition'[22] that was conceived either for performance as a ballet or as a concerto for piano and eighteen instruments. The occasion for which *Aubade* was commissioned was billed as a *'bal des Matières'* to which guests were to wear costumes made of some 'primary material': Marie-Laure herself wore a costume made predominantly of holly, her husband sported a suit cut in oilcloth, Valentine Hugo arrived fetchingly clad in a dress made of napkins, Paul Morand's suit was festooned with the covers of his books, while Maurice Sachs, most uncomfortably for himself and his dancing partners, wore a costume somehow fashioned out of pebbles. There were various musical and other interludes in the course of the evening, the centre-piece being Poulenc's ballet, choreographed by Nijinska, costumes and *décor* by Jean-Michel Frank (who at an earlier *bal masqué* on the theme of Parisian personalities had appeared resplendent in one of Marie-Laure's own numerous ball-gowns) and with Poulenc himself as the featured soloist on piano. 'A ballet on the chastity of Diana', the programme of *Aubade* was devised by the composer and consisted, in his own words, of the following narrative elements:

> At sunrise, surrounded by her female companions, Diana rebels against the divine law that condemns her to perpetual virginity (*pureté*). Her companions console her, and restore her sense of divinity by presenting her with her bow. Diana seizes it sadly, then leaps into the forest, seeking, in the hunt, an outlet (*dérivatif*) for her amorous torments.

> ECR p. 80

Divided into eight movements and lasting about 20 minutes in all, *Aubade* displays a far greater musical and emotional complexity than any previous work Poulenc had written, and its shifts in mood from melancholy to manic hyperactivity and back to something approaching anguish are clearly expressive of some deep conflict within the composer himself who, as featured pianist, is identified very closely with the figure of Diana.[23] The whole point of *Aubade* is that the dawn it evokes proves to be a false dawn, a failure on the part of the goddess-heroine to resolve the questions raised by her thwarted sexuality, and, culminates, to the accompaniment of music of genuine anguish, in her fleeing the light of day and rushing desperately into the forest, bow in hand, to seek an 'outlet', in violence, for the 'amorous torments' she can neither satisfy nor deny; the whole work has a distraught, almost hysterical quality that must greatly have clashed with the general mood of the de Noailles' *soirée*. That what Rostand called the work's 'poetico-erotic element' was of great importance to Poulenc is shown by the composer's anger and dismay, still evident 25 years after the event, that when *Aubade* was given its first public performance on 21 January the following year at the Théâtre des Champs-Elyseés, the new choreographer, George Balanchine, altered the scenario, with Poulenc's reluctant permission, to incorporate the story of Diana and Actaeon. To Poulenc, speaking in 1954, the presence of a male dancer introduced a wholly discordant element into what he had conceived as 'a *ballet de femmes*, of feminine solitude' (ECR p. 81). Poulenc's objections were almost certainly not merely, or even primarily, aesthetic, though precisely which psychological nerve was exposed by the change in the scenario is difficult to pinpoint. Did it make the identification of the composer-pianist with the sexually frustrated goddess too explicit, or did the presence of a male body on stage betray all too obviously his true object of desire? Diana's tragedy is both that her love has destroyed her divine self-sufficiency and that, forbidden by divine (paternal) decree, her passion is condemned to remain forever unsatisfied. Though its sexual allegory is fuzzy at best, *Aubade* is clearly the work of a divided and unhappy individual whose inner conflicts are tearing him apart, just as surely as Actaeon will be torn limb from limb by Diana's staghounds for the unforgivable crime of having *seen*. *Aubade*, Poulenc insisted, was not just a 'tragedy' (C p. 313), it was a 'wound' ('*une blessure*', C p. 300). Despite manifold weaknesses of structure and argument, Poulenc had discovered an artistic strategy to which he would frequently have recourse for making his most personal utterances, above all in *Dialogues des Carmélites* and *La Voix humaine*: it is a female figure, chaste, frustrated or abandoned, that he delegates to voice his deepest divisions and miseries. Unhappy, repressed, troubled throughout his life by his sexual duality to which divine decree denied legitimate fulfilment, the *moine* that lurked beneath Poulenc's *voyou* exterior was almost fated to find his fullest expression in a tragedy about nuns and their sacrificial death on the scaffold.

The completion, and relative success, of *Aubade* had a cathartic influence on Poulenc and, in November 1929, he described himself to Claire Croiza as having been 'resuscitated' after the protracted miseries of 1928 (C p. 317). Then, just as he seemed to be 'becoming once more the Poulenc that you knew with, deep inside me, a hidden sensitivity (*une sensibilité cacheé*) which, I think, does my music no harm at all' (C p. 316), the first of many future guillotine blades fell with the utterly unexpected death (from peritonitis, after the briefest of illnesses) of Raymonde Linossier on 30 January 1930; she was buried with the manuscript of *Les Biches* in her hands. It is scarcely an exaggeration that Poulenc grieved for Raymonde for the rest of his life. He reputedly placed a photograph of her on the bedside table of every hotel he ever stayed in (C p. 326), and took a cigarette case she had owned to every important performance of his work he attended (C p. 548). He claimed frequently to experience the 'feeling of a double presence in me' (C p. 519), as though inhabited still by the ghost of the one woman he had loved but to whom he never said '*tu*'. Raymonde Linossier, in short, was an unattainable anima-figure or goddess whom, six years later at Rocamadour, and forever thereafter, Poulenc may unconsciously have conflated with the inscrutable figure, both distant and close, of the Black Madonna (see the fourth chapter, 'Black Virgin: Poulenc at Rocamadour'). Finally, to cap all his woes, Poulenc lost a substantial amount of money in the aftermath of the Wall Street *débâcle*, and would never again be able to live the kind of life he had come to expect on unearned income alone; henceforth, he would have to perform, as well as compose, in order to make a reasonable living. As the 1930s began, with economic and political crisis already in the air, Poulenc may not yet have been ripe for conversion, but at the heart of his life there was – Chanlaire notwithstanding – a sense of emptiness and frustration that, in certain circumstances, might make him look to the Church into which he had been born for whatever it was that artistic and social success had so far failed to deliver.

Homosexuality, Catholicism and modernism

The path that led Poulenc into the Church in the late 1930s had been trodden by many French writers, artists and intellectuals over the previous half century, and his 'conversion' – for that is what it was, in the sense that it transformed him from a nominal into a committed Roman Catholic – can only be fully understood in the context of a much wider movement of minds. In the wake of France's crushing military defeat by Prussia in 1870-71, and of the ensuing social and political upheaval of the Paris Commune and its bloody repression (March–May 1871), there began what has been well described as a 'reactionary revolution'[24] in which the Catholic Church in France, inspired from 'across the mountains' (whence the term 'Ultramontanism' to designate the whole of the movement) by the example of the beleaguered Pope Pius IX in the Vatican, sought to reverse the spread of democracy, liberalism and secularism which it believed to have been unleashed by that ultimate work of the Devil, the French Revolution. From the mid-1870s until 1905, when Church and State were finally separated, the Catholic Church (or at least its dominant wing) fought a bitter, and ultimately unsuccessful, Thirty Years' War against modernity in all of its forms, enlisting in its struggle every ideological weapon it could muster, from royalism in the 1870s to extreme anti-Semitism at the time of the Dreyfus Affair (1894-9). It was the great age of pilgrimages, Marian apparitions and the burgeoning cult of the Sacred Heart of Jesus, marmorealised in the huge basilica of that name on the Butte de Montmartre which glowered out at the Eiffel Tower, a symbol of the detested modern world, erected on the other side of the Seine in 1889 to commemorate the centenary of the storming of the Bastille and the proclamation of the Rights of Man, every one of which was anathema to the Ultramontanist camp. In the teeth of modern science, the Church promoted the mass pilgrimage to Lourdes, inspired by the Marian apparition of 1858, while its most extreme wing countered progressivism with the apocalyptic prophecies made by the Virgin to two peasant children at La Salette in the French Alps in 1846, prophecies that Léon Bloy, the most extreme of the extremists, and, after him, Jacques Maritain made the guiding inspiration of their lives; rationalism was confounded with the example of stigmatics like Catherine Emmerich (1774-1824) and Louise Lateau (1850-83), and the life and death of 'Petite Fleur', Sister (later Saint) Thérèse de l'Enfant Jésus et de la Sainte Face (1873-97) which were held up as the very model for Catholics to follow. Even when urged in 1892 by a new Pope, Leo XIII, to 'rally' to the Republic, many French Catholics, including most of its intellectual converts, continued to regard democracy and its associated values (liberalism, humanism, rationalism, secularism) as Satanic inventions. God, taunted one of their opponents, had been transformed into a political figure who sat on the far right of the French Chamber of Deputies – with, he might have added, the Virgin Mary placed even further to the right of the right hand of the Father.

The reactionary revolution was a revolution of the *élite*, above all of the intellectual and artistic *élite* who rapidly emerged as its militant vanguard. Conversion followed conversion, and between the mid-1880s and the outbreak of war in 1914, a whole succession of talented writers and artists rallied openly to the Church and committed their minds and work to its cause, commonly taking up positions more radical than those of the official Church hierarchy and certainly more so than those of the average practising Catholic. Claudel (who underwent a life-transforming spiritual experience at Notre-Dame on Christmas Day 1886, at the age of 18) was probably the most formidable figure, to be followed, in no particular order of chronology or importance, by the novelist Joris-Karl Huysmans (1848-1907), author of the Bible of decadence, *A rebours* (1884), and the satanistic *Là-bas* (1891), who returned to the church in the mid-1890s, Charles Péguy (1873-1914), founder of the great Easter pilgrimage to Chartres and one of the few Catholic intellectuals of the period not to veer to the far right, Ernest Psichari (1883-1914) who converted to Catholicism whilst serving in the French colonial army in North Africa and who, like Péguy, was killed in the first weeks of the war, and Jacques Rivière (1886-1925), secretary and then director of the *Nouvelle Revue Française* and, as such, one of the most influential figures in France before typhoid fever destroyed him, like Radiguet, in his prime. Other leading figures of the Catholic revival – not strictly converts in that they never distanced themselves from the Church of their birth – were the painter Georges Rouault (1871-1958), another link in the network that spread out from Bloy, and Georges Bernanos (1888-1948), author of the posthumous *Dialogues des Carmélites* (1949) who, like many French Catholics of the time, including many priests, espoused the cause of the proto-fascist Action Française until the spectacle of Francoist violence in the Spanish Civil War – often committed by Muslim legionnaires in the name of 'Catholic civilisation' – drew him back, after much turmoil, into the democratic camp. The Catholicism of such men, and of the suffering women from whom they often took inspiration, was a Catholicism of sacrifice, martyrdom and death, a Catholicism suffused in the blood of the Cross, in which suffering and pain were voluntarily accepted, even actively sought (Huysmans, for example, refused any treatment or alleviating drugs for the mouth cancer that killed him), so as to deflect God's anger from unbelieving France and thus redeem – in the literal sense of 'ransoming' or 'buying back' with the coin, if necessary, of blood sacrifice – its people from the clutches of Satan who held the contemporary world in his thrall. If the French people as a whole would not believe, pray and suffer for Christ, then it was the duty of the surviving Catholic remnant to believe, pray, suffer and, if need be, die in their place and on their behalf. Thus was born the teaching of 'vicarious suffering' or 'mystical substitution' which, luridly promoted by Huysmans and Bloy in both their lives and their works, resurfaces as the theological core of *Dialogues des Carmélites* 30 years and more after their deaths.

Following their conversion by Bloy in 1905, it was Jacques and Raïssa Maritain who, after his death, took over his role as the crucial link in the whole Catholic intellectual network in France.[25] First at Versailles and then, after 1923, at Meudon just to the south-west of Paris, where their house at No. 10 Rue du Parc had its own private consecrated chapel, the Maritains lived together 'as brother and sister', having renounced sexual relations with each other by solemn oath taken in Versailles Cathedral in 1912, and devoted their lives to prayer, reading and writing (Jacques soon became the leading Catholic philosopher in France, responsible almost singlehandedly for the great revival in the study of medieval scholasticism) and securing the conversions of as many prominent French writers, intellectuals and artists as they could. With the help of numerous associates, both clerical and lay, they transformed No. 10 Rue du Parc into a kind of conversion machine in which invited guests were cajoled, incited and sometimes bullied into becoming communicating members of the Church, with Jacques providing the intellectual, and Raïssa the emotional, ammunition; had she not left Russia and become a Catholic convert, Raïssa, Maurice Sachs believed, would have made a first-rate Stalinist apparatchik. Significantly, one of their earliest 'successes', even before they came to Meudon, was the writer Henri Ghéon (1875-1944), a regular cruising companion of Gide both in Paris and North Africa, who 'returned' to the Church in 1915-16, became a member of Action Française, and devoted himself henceforth to writing modern mystery plays like *Les Trois Miracles de Sainte Cécile* (1919) and *Job* (1932) for performance by the 'faithful' in parish halls up and down France; he seriously compromised himself under the Vichy regime.[26] Homosexuals were not targeted as such by the Meudon conversion machine, but it is with the story of the botched conversions of Jean Cocteau and Maurice Sachs that we can best begin our exploration of the curious links between homosexuality, Catholicism and modernism in inter-war France.

'In three days I am to be executed by God's firing squad.' (*'Dans trois jours je serai fusillé par les soldats de Dieu.'*) When, three days after uttering these extraordinary words, Raymond Radiguet did indeed die, alone, aged 20, in a Parisian clinic on 12 December 1923, Cocteau, who could not bear to see his corpse or to attend his funeral, felt, in his own words, that he had been 'operated on without chloroform', amputated, as it were, of half, or more than half, of his physical and spiritual being.[27] Distraught with grief, *le veuf* (widower) *sur le toit*, as unkind wits immediately dubbed him, accompanied Poulenc and Auric to Monte-Carlo in January 1924 to attend the premieres of their respective ballets, *Les Biches* and *Les Fâcheux*, and it was there that he was introduced to the music critic Louis Laloy (1874-1943) who, in his turn, introduced Cocteau (and his two friends) to the consolations and pleasures of opium; that the proselytising author of *Le Livre de la fumeé* (1913) was also affiliated to the Maritain circle (and a resident of Meudon to boot) offers further evidence of the extraordinary interconnectedness of the artistic and intellectual life of the period. But, in his misery, Cocteau turned not only to opium but to God ('I was asking for mercy. It was so simple to ask for grace'), and wrote to his friend, fellow homosexual and Christian convert, Max Jacob, at Saint-Benoît-sur-Loire and was urged to confess and take communion 'the way one goes to a doctor'. 'What?' Cocteau wrote back, 'you advise me to swallow the Host like an aspirin tablet?' Only to receive the disarming reply: 'The Host must be taken like an aspirin tablet.' But, eschewing both aspirin and communion wafer in favour of opium, Cocteau was soon heavily addicted, smoking up to ten pipefuls per day (three at nine in the morning, four at five in the afternoon and three at eleven in the evening) and, in June 1924, readily accepted when Auric offered to take him to Meudon to receive spiritual counsel from the Maritains. The Maritains, in their turn, were both genuinely concerned for Cocteau's well-being and anxious to secure his conversion as part of their grand strategy of rechristianising the French intellectual and artistic *élite*. However sincere Cocteau might be in his quest for spiritual wholeness (according to Sachs, he spoke continually of Maritain and God, though not, to be fair, in that order),[28] formal membership of the Church was a more complicated matter entirely. At Maritain's insistence, he agreed to tackle the immediate obstacle, and in February 1915 entered a detoxification clinic located, with admirable symbolism, on the corner of the Rues de Chateaubriand and Lord-Byron in the eighth *arrondissement*, remaining there for six weeks, supposedly in complete isolation but in fact – and here was the second, and much deeper, problem – receiving secret visits from the 19-year-old Jean Bourgoint (1905-66) whom he had met just before entering the clinic and to whom he had, as he put it, given 'his first whiff of opium in a kiss'.[29]

On his discharge at the end of April, Cocteau resumed not just his double addiction to opium and young men, but also his visits to Meudon where the Maritains redoubled their efforts to convert him. On the evening of 15 June 1925, Cocteau was about to leave one such meeting when there arrived at 10 Rue du Parc, almost as though pre-arranged by the Maritains or by some higher agency still, one of the more remarkable members of their circle. Father Charles Henrion was a pre-war convert – one of Claudel's many 'conquests' – whom the Maritains had known since 1913 and who, at the time of his serendipitous arrival, was permanently based in Tunisia where, along with another convert, the former Admiral Malcor, he had founded the Confraternity of Sidi-Saad, a contemplative order that also provided medical care for the local population. A devotee of the latter-day desert hermit Father Charles de Foucauld (1858-1916) (who had died a martyr's death deep in the Sahara, at Tamanrasset in Algeria, in December 1916), Père Charles, as he was always known, arrived wearing a white *burnous* emblazoned with the emblem that Foucauld had reputedly devised to stop the infidels in their tracks, a blood-red Sacred Heart surmounted by a crimson cross. It certainly worked its magic on Cocteau who was, in his own words, knocked out by the sudden and, to him, preternatural apparition, and, while he was still 'groggy' (his word, in English), Jacques and Raïssa, together with the rest of the Meudon conversion machine, moved in for their most important 'killing' to date. Two days later, after a thorough working-over by Maritain and the recently converted poet Pierre Reverdy (1889-1960), Cocteau was whisked upstairs to the private chapel where Père Charles heard his confession, following which, on Friday 19 June 1925, he took communion for the first time since adolescence, in the presence not only of the Maritains but, it is piquant to observe, of fellow homosexual Henri Ghéon. Still 'groggy' no doubt, 'JC' had been swiftly and safely delivered into the welcoming arms of 'J-C': Cocteau always liked 'coincidences' like that.[30] A convert, Maritain would famously write in his open letter to Cocteau the following year, is 'a man whom God has turned inside out like a glove. All the seams are outside, the leather (*l'écorce*) is inside, it no longer has any use.'[31] Cocteau's life had certainly been shaken, even shattered, since Radiguet's death, but had it truly been 'turned inside out'?

Cocteau's immediate response was that of any writer: to write. Begun in August 1925 and published along with Maritain's *réponse* the following year, his *Lettre à Jacques Maritain* gave a highly dramatic account of the circumstances of his conversion, and committed its author to the cause of 'Art for God's sake' and notably failed to condemn or foreswear the smoking of opium – though it did concede that 'opium resembles religion to the extent that an illusionist resembles Jesus'. Not only did Cocteau continue to smoke opium, but it seems likely that he sometimes – notably at Midnight Mass at Meudon at the end of the year – took communion under its influence.[32] In addition, he pursued his relationship with Jean Bourgoint whom he persuaded – either by way of squaring his own conscience or in order to entangle his lover in the same moral dilemmas as himself – to be baptised in August 1925. After a highly colourful and erratic existence, Bourgoint was admitted to the Trappist monastery at Cîteaux as a lay brother in 1947 and remained there for 16 years as Frère Pascal, dividing his time between dairy, laundry and the study of theology, before having himself transferred to Cameroon where, a true holy fool, he worked in a leper colony at Mokolo, 'the poorest village in the world', as he called it, making orthopaedic footware for sufferers of leprosy of the feet, and dying there of cancer in 1966.[33] Cocteau's Catholicism was far less enduring. A man of the theatre who lived his 'private' life in public, he could hardly remain immune to the accusations of hypocrisy that soon fell upon him. On his 'return to the sacraments' Père Charles had urged him to 'remain free' (*'rester libre'*), words which Cocteau, to Maritain's dismay, interpreted as meaning that he could do – and, above all, publish – what he liked. Maritain soon had to ask him to withdraw his long poem *L'Ange Heurtebise* – written before his conversion and celebrating with lyrical bravado his passion for Radiguet – from its projected publication in the Meudon circle's literary collection. Cocteau would not compromise and, publishing his poem elsewhere, distanced himself from the Maritains without, however, breaking with them completely. In July 1927, Maritain wrote to Cocteau explaining how, in the eyes of the Church, homosexual love, however passionate and sincere, is an infraction of both the divine and the natural order and, as such, 'a profound refusal of the Cross', to which Cocteau replied that he 'needed love and to make love to souls', scarcely bothering to conceal that he preferred such souls to be enclosed in a beautiful masculine physique.[34]

The beginning of the end came in February 1928 when Cocteau contributed a rapturous preface to the first published work, provocatively entitled *J'adore*, by his latest companion Jean Desbordes (1906-44). To add insult to the injury he was knowingly inflicting on the Maritains, Cocteau's words appear alongside a photo-portrait of Desbordes wearing a sailor suit. *J'adore* is a collection of homosexual fantasies and confessions, parts of which seem to have been written – possibly with Cocteau's aid and encouragement – deliberately to offend and antagonise the Maritains. Here, for example, is Desbordes's gay anti-credo:

> I declare that the Holy Sacrament which is a loving presence exists in affection. I declare that when this miraculous affection brings together two beings, to the point of causing them to die for each other, the divine presence is no longer in the church, but in the lovers' soul [...] Jacques Maritain murmurs that human love is a disfigured, violated love, grace betrayed. Love is royal. It reigns over the many Versailles of the heart. It stops Satan as fire stops wild beasts.[35]

This mixing of 'God and the genitals' was too much for Maritain, and though he told Cocteau he was not judging Desbordes ('I leave that to God'), 'it is a question of knowing whether masturbation and homosexual love (*l'onanisme et l'amour pédérastique*) form an appropriate reliquary for the Names of Jesus, the Virgin and the saints.'[36] 'Maritain thinks that Jean [Desbordes] is a devil in disguise,' Cocteau retorted to an American friend. 'He is mistaken. Jean is a love.'[37] The following June, Maritain learned that Cocteau was about to publish, albeit anonymously and in a limited edition of 31 copies, an explicit account and defence of his homosexual experiences entitled *Le Livre blanc*, and again he wrote to the author urging him to withdraw it: 'This project belongs to the Devil. It is the first time that you have made a public act of adhesion to evil.' Refusing once more to comply, Cocteau made a resolute defence of artistic and personal freedom: 'Follow your road without compromise and let me follow my own. In imitating yours I would distort myself and distort human beings as they are.'[38] *Le Livre blanc* was published, in which he affirmed both his homosexuality and his faith, ending his apologia on a courageous note of defiance: 'A vice of society makes my uprightness (*droiture*) a vice. I am withdrawing. In France, this vice does not lead to prison on account of Cambacérès's proclivities and the longevity of the Code Napoléon. But I will not accept being tolerated. That offends my love of love and of liberty.'[39]

And that, more or less, was that. After undergoing a further detoxification cure, Cocteau tried to re-establish contact with No. 10 Rue du Parc, but the Maritains had had enough, and they would maintain only the most formal relationship with Cocteau thereafter. In retrospect, the whole business seems a tragic blunder on both sides, with the Maritains, for good reasons and bad, putting undue pressure on an individual whose emotional vulnerability and taste for the theatrical led him to take a step against which the slightest self-knowledge should have forewarned him. How can either party have seriously supposed that Cocteau would have been able – even if he had been willing, which he was not – to contain his artistic and personal freedom within the moral straightjacket of the Church? And when it came, as it inevitably must, to choosing between the opium pipe and the 'aspirin' of the Host, or, still more, if it may so be put, between JB (Bourgoint), JD (Desbordes) and J-C, can either proselytisers or proselytised have doubted which way JC would jump? The only individuals to emerge with credit from the affair are, ironically, Bourgoint and Desbordes, both of them authentic martyrs to their respective beliefs, Bourgoint in the circumstances described, Desbordes as an agent for the Polish Resistance tortured to death by the Gestapo in July 1944, as the Maritains prepared to return from America in honour and while Cocteau, with typical slipperiness, endeavoured to cover up his equivocal career in occupied Paris.[40]

If Cocteau's botched conversion mingled pathos, posturing and an alarming lack of insight on all sides, that of his one-time companion and secretary, Maurice Sachs, was a typically grotesque episode in a life of self-destructive dissipation that ended in horror and ignominy in Germany in April 1945. Born in 1906 into a Jewish family which, in his own words, 'married and divorced with incredible vivacity'[41], Sachs seems not to have known his father and was brought up by his spendthrift mother, aided and abetted by the first wife of her father (not her mother), who had later married Jacques Bizet, son of the composer, dandy, alcoholic and opiomane, whose life and death (by suicide in 1922) seem deadly harbingers of Sachs's own. After a Catholic schooling and early initiation into drugs and homosexuality, Sachs was, by his mid-teens, a familiar figure in the whirl of post-war Parisian nightlife, meeting Cocteau, as it was almost fated that he would, in February 1924. The pudgy-faced Sachs had little to commend him as a sexual partner, but Cocteau adopted him as one of his *gosses*, using him as a combined secretary, errand boy and sounding board for his wit. Cocteau later described Sachs as 'a cameleon, stricken with the disease of mimeticism', and it seems indeed to have been partly in emulation and envy of his mentor that Sachs set foot on his own singularly ill-advised road to Meudon-Damascus. Like Cocteau, Sachs was in the throes of emotional turmoil, and the Church seemed likely to fulfil the 'desire for a framework' that he was always seeking and then rebelling against. In July, Sachs begged Cocteau to guide him into the Church ('Jean, lead me, you who bear the initials of the saviour (*vous qui avez les initiales divines*)'). Cocteau gave his name to the Maritains and, on 1 August, Sachs duly made his way to Meudon. There he was received with the customary courtesy and concern, and – remember he was not yet 19 – felt himself 'melt and become small and quite child-like' before Jacques's Christ-like mien. Having arrived friendless and forlorn, he left feeling he had found nothing less than a Messiah, though whether that was Jesus or Jacques – or, for that matter, Oedipus or his true self – it would take him many years to decide. On the train back to Paris, he decided to be 'REUNITED with humanity' in the form of '300 million Catholics', overwhelmed with joy at having at long last discovered an 'oasis', a 'warm inn', in which he could be at one with 'the *eternal* father, the *virgin* mother and the son who had *sacrificed* himself for me'. As with Cocteau, the Maritains were anxious to expedite Sachs's entry into the Church, and recommended him to another priest in their circle, the aptly named Père Pressoir ('Father Winepress'), director of the Carmelite seminary in Paris. After little more than a month of instruction, Sachs was baptised in the chapel at No. 10 Rue du Parc on 29 August, having, according to his baptismal certificate, formally 'renounced the errors of the Jews' and adopted the principle of *nulla salus extra ecclesiam*, with Jacques, Raïssa and Cocteau (although he was not present at the ceremony) acting as godparents. First communion and confirmation followed almost immediately: another triumph, if a minor one, for the celestial conversion machine, though not without Raïssa's confiding to her diary her disquiet concerning 'something obscure' in the most recently acquired of her godsons. Thus far, no harm, and possibly some good, had been done, and matters might have rested there had not Sachs, through a mixture of post-conversion euphoria, guilt, pride and a desire to emulate the holiness of the Maritains and Pressoir, decided that being an ordinary practising Catholic was not enough and that he was being called to a higher religious vocation. With what seems a culpable lack of psychological, let alone spiritual, discernment, the Maritains, with Cocteau in support, encouraged Sachs to pursue his vocation, and on 2 January 1926 he entered the Carmelite house on the Rue d'Assas in the sixth *arrondissement*. For the first few weeks things went passably well, and Sachs was able to receive cigarettes and other creature comforts *ad libitum*. As a special concession, elicited by Jacques, the neophyte was permitted to wear a cassock from the outset; reputedly, Sachs had one run up by Chanel, and took great delight in hitching it up 'like a young woman' as he went up the altar steps to take Holy Communion. But soon 'the struggles between Jacob and the Angel' began with a vengeance, and all the hair shirts, spiked iron bracelets and scourges in the seminary could not quell the clamourings of sexual desire; each night's prayers swarmed with masturbatory fantasies and the fantasies won, and in July 1926, after Maritain's intervention, Sachs was granted leave of absence to go on holiday with his 'grandmother'. If Sachs's superiors thought that Mme Bizet would preserve her charge from temptation, they were grievously in error, for grandson and 'grandmother' headed directly for Juan-les-Pins, then just establishing itself as an ultra-fashionable resort, where Sachs met and fell madly in love with an American teenager named Tom Pinkerton with whom, wearing a pink bathing-costume under his cassock, he promenaded hand in hand on the beach.[42] Pinkerton's mother wrote a letter of protest to the Bishop of Nice, and Sachs was sent back to Paris via Solesmes and a stay with Jacob at Saint-Benoît-sur-Loire; to his very considerable relief, Père Pressoir refused to re-admit him into the seminary, telling him that it would be much better for him to be a good Christian than a bad priest. With desire and devotion vying within him, Sachs continued to practise (with Maritain's encouragement, though his wife seems to have suspended relations with him entirely) until finally the conflict became too much for him to bear; in one of his last desperate letters to Jacques he describes how, on his knees at Benediction one evening, he was reduced to gnawing the chair in front of him 'because the Blessed Sacrament sent me into a state of terrible rage. I think of God with FEAR and REVOLT'. Then, in November 1926, military service took him out of

France, out of the Church and out of the Maritains' life, pending further adventures, humiliations and deceptions. His end was predictably sordid. After playing the black market[43] and informing for the Gestapo in occupied Paris, Sachs tried in desperation to pre-empt deportation by volunteering as a labourer in Germany. Working as a crane operator in Hamburg, he continued to spy and inform on fellow foreign workers until his arrest and imprisonment in November 1943 for black-market and other illicit activities. Though known to be Jewish, he managed to survive in prison for almost a year and a half, trading information on other prisoners for drugs, food and writing materials. As the Allies advanced, the inmates were forced marched in the direction of Kiel, an ordeal which proved too much for Sachs; unable to continue, he was taken to one side and dispatched with a bullet in the back of his head.

Cocteau and Sachs were in and out of the Church within two or three years and, though neither was exactly prime conversion 'material', their tribulations were evidence of the extreme difficulty, if not outright impossibility, of being both an active Catholic and an active homosexual at the time, especially if one's director of conscience was a man as exacting as Jacques Maritain. Two other homosexual converts, Max Jacob and Julien Green (1900-98), *did* remain in the Church but at the price, in both cases, of self-lacerating guilt, perpetual evasiveness and spiritual anguish, with Jacob, in particular, living in constant dread of eternal damnation and seeking refuge in Saint-Benoît-sur-Loire as much from his own homosexuality as from the pettiness and in-fighting of literary Paris. Following his initial vision of Christ on the bedroom wall of his lodgings in Montmartre in 1909 (see the first chapter) – confirmed in December 1914 by a second vision in a cinema in Montparnasse – Jacob had repeated nightmares in one of which a divine emissary descends from a flying chariot to announce that, 'Max Jacob has lost the right to happiness on earth and in heaven. He does not know what he is losing!'[44] Often bored and depressed in Saint-Benoît, despite making daily confession and communion, Jacob returned to Paris in 1928, took up lodgings on the Rue Nollet in Montmartre from which base close to the notorious amusement arcade in the Place de Clichy (see the first chapter) he lived what is loosely described as a 'life of dissipation' until, consumed with self-disgust, he returned to Saint-

Benoît in 1937 from which only the arrival of the Gestapo in February 1944 could remove him: the hell to which he had feared that God would consign him turned out, in the end, to be an entirely human contrivance.

Of American parents, but brought up in France, Julien Green converted from Protestantism to Catholicism shortly after the death of his mother in 1916 and, until later life, was notably cagey about his sexual orientation, finally 'coming out' in his fourth volume of autobiography *Jeunesse* (1974), having the previous year decided to re-publish his novel *Le Malfaiteur* (written 1936-8, first published 1955) complete with the plainly autobiographical homosexual 'confession' by its principal character, Jean, that he had earlier thought prudent to suppress. In Green's case, horror at his own homosexuality was, by his own admission, translated into a horror of sexuality as such: '*It was sexuality as a whole that I refused*, whether or not it was that of the majority.'[45] Accordingly, the (hetero)sexual obsessiveness that haunts early novels such as *Adrienne Mesurat* (1927) and *Léviathan* (1928), with their claustrophobic atmosphere shot through with the threat of madness and violence, is commonly interpreted as a refraction of Green's inability to reconcile his homosexuality with his faith. A 'phobia of the sexual act', heterosexual and homosexual alike, runs like a leitmotiv through the whole of his work, and rarely have homosexual encounters on station forecourts and streets been described with greater desolation and metaphysical horror than in 'La Confession de Jean':

> You cannot imagine what is concealed beneath those words: to run after pleasure (*courir après le plaisir*), the sadness of the endless avenues along which one wanders all night long, year after year, the disappointments, the dangers, the solitude. Lay all the streets of the world end to end, they lead to hell, yes, they make you believe in hell.[46]

In his misery, Jean, a Derek Jarman *avant la lettre*, undertakes a study of the iconography of Saint Sebastian over the centuries. Young and beautiful, Sebastian is 'Apollo resuscitated on the altars of Christianity', Dionysos reborn in all his erotic glory before being transfixed by the institutionalised arrows of a homophobic Church: 'Hands bound, his look sometimes sad sometimes shifty (*sournois*), he is the image of that ineradicable love that the Christian church has sought to wipe off the face of the earth.'[47]

By the time Poulenc returned to the Church in the late 1930s, the 'reactionary revolution' was in temporary abeyance following the 1926 papal ban on Catholic membership of Action Française, though Catholic support for Franco's supposed defence of 'Catholic civilisation' in Spain was almost universal: amongst leading Catholic writers, only Mauriac, Bernanos and ... Maritain denounced the idea of an 'anti-atheistic', 'anti-communist' crusade. Nothing had changed, of course, in the Church's attitude towards homosexuality. Though decriminalised since 1791, sodomy and other homosexual acts were still 'sins that cried out to heaven for vengeance', and in 1937 the French Church was rocked from top to bottom when Monseigneur Joseph Marcadé, Bishop of Laval, was suspended from his functions after being discovered in the traditional 'compromising position' with a group of cadets at the nearby military academy – the French Sandhurst, no less – of Saumur.[48] Why, then, given the unyielding hostility of the Church to their sexual orientation (let alone to the sexual acts it might lead them to commit), did a significant number of homosexual writers and intellectuals opt for membership of the Church between the two wars? 'Explanations' in this area will probably say as much about the would-be explainer as about the matter to be explained. There will be those, no doubt, who point to the aesthetic appeal of Catholic ritual as a reason, proverbially frilly vestments and soothing 'smells and bells' in the most trivial versions, not forgetting the perennial topos of cherubic choirboys who are rather less innocent than they look ...[49] The more psychoanalytically inclined will stress the indisputable fact that, of the homosexual converts discussed here, three lost their fathers whilst still very young (Cocteau's committed suicide in 1898 when Cocteau was nine, Sachs never knew his, Poulenc's died when he was 17) whilst Green and his father were 'almost two strangers towards each other' from his earliest years. 'Mother problems' could have played a part: Poulenc's and Green's died when they were in their teens, Cocteau's was fussy and over-protective, while Sachs's was (by his account) an appalling mixture of dissipation and bigotry, leading him to the wry reflection that, 'if ever the Catholic Church had a miraculous inspiration, it was in promulgating the doctrine of the Virginity of the Mother of Christ, for the purity of his mother is a fiction which every man longs to believe.'[50] It is also indisputable that Cocteau, Sachs and Poulenc converted at a time of great emotional vulnerability, with the death of a lover (Cocteau) and, as we shall see, of an esteemed musical colleague (Poulenc) being the precipitating factor in at least two of the cases. Cocteau and Sachs openly admitted their need for an ethical and institutional framework, and it has been argued (by Robert Merle in the existentialist 'house journal' *Les Temps modernes* in 1954) that their respective conversions were 'an attempt on the part of men who felt themselves outlawed by society on account of their homosexuality to rejoin the human community and expiate their sense of guilt by adhering precisely to that system which most rigidly rejected their sexual orientation'[51] – classic instances, in other words, of Sartrean inauthenticity and bad faith.

The trouble with such 'explanations' is that most of them can be applied equally to heterosexual and homosexual converts. It is difficult to imagine two men more responsive to ecclesiastical architecture and ritual than Claudel or, from his different perspective as a theatre designer, Jean Hugo, yet both were heterosexuals, and both also had difficult and distant fathers – as, for that matter, did Maritain whose father expelled his wife, young daughter and virtually new-born son from the conjugal household in 1883. Similarly, Hugo converted in 1931 after he and his artist wife, Valentine, divorced in 1929 and she became the very public companion of André Breton himself; Ernest Psichari converted after attempting suicide when Maritain's sister rejected his proposals of marriage. Finally, no two people can have wanted a moral and intellectual framework more desperately than Jacques and Raïssa Maritain who, as a young married couple made a solemn vow and promise (in the Jardin des Plantes in Paris) that they would commit joint suicide if, within a given time, they had not found a philosophically satisfactory reason for living; a few months later they made contact with Bloy. What is certain, however, is that, at the moment that he made the crucial decision to (re-) enter the Church, each of the gay converts examined in this chapter, even the feckless and mendacious Sachs, felt either a strong faith, or a strong need for faith, and that, feeling as he did, he either failed to read the 'small print' of the spiritual contract he was signing or, if he did, felt that he could overcome, or evade, the obstacle of his sexual orientation. The idea that Jacob, Cocteau and the rest became Catholics in order to flee or deny their sexuality, or to suffer even more because of it than they had done so far, is, on the available evidence, quite simply unsustainable. There are, in short, no specifically 'gay' reasons for converting; there is only the far deeper mystery of conversion itself.

Once within the Church, however, the gay converts in question may have had a particular, if still not wholly distinctive, way of living their Catholicism. Reading their works, one is struck by the centrality for them of the Body of Christ, either in respect of its Real Presence in the sacrament or, more particularly, as it was presented to them daily, splayed, bleeding and abandoned on the Cross. Concerning the former, Green describes how, in the early 1920s, after a night's cruising, he would frequently go the Chapel of the Soeurs Blanches on the Rue Cortambert in the sixteenth *arrondissement*, where he had been baptised a Catholic in 1916, and there join the sisters kneeling in adoration before the Blessed Sacrament displayed in its ostensory. 'There was the Presence, above all, mysteriously perceptible within these walls', but, still more than that, there were the sisters themselves kneeling in the 'magical immobility of time, transformed into statues before the snow-white Host, that impenetrable silence'.[52] Kneeling beside them, the young man identifies as much with the sisters as with the consecrated wafer in the monstrance before him. Similarly, it may be significant that Poulenc's exquisite 1952 setting of the 'Ave Verum Corpus' is for female voices only: the composer as it were feminises himself in the Real Presence of Christ. Finally, it is surely no coincidence that Sachs's eventual hostility towards the Church was directed at the Blessed Sacrament itself (see above): the Body of Christ was too central to his Catholicism not to be rejected with a display of oral aggression and fear.

But the focus of 'gay Catholicism' was undoubtedly the figure of Christ on the Cross. The reality of the martyred male body is, as we shall see, the central mystery of Poulenc's Catholicism, as it was of that of Jacob, whose fate it was to become that martyred body himself. Here, for example, is part of Jacob's remarkable 'Mise au tombeau' ('The Entombment'), published in

1919, four years after his reception into the Church:

> Your (*ton*) dead body! to have loved it so much when it was alive! but still stone-like flesh is still yours, my beloved! My God! there is still blood on his pretty forehead: it all seems to sweat but is nonetheless hard. It is your corpse! my pretty God (*mon Dieu joli*) reduced to a corpse. [...] Your belly is hard too: that is the most surprising thing about corpses. I had never seen how delicate your feet are. [...] Alas! I have never felt how much I love you since your death: I am in love with your corpse and I see how much I loved you without realising I did. [...] Here are your pierced feet. Oh! the swine! how they made you suffer: they pierced you, you, God, you a more than charming young man, more than seductive, more than genial. That unique marvel, God descended to earth, they destroyed it in their wrath.[53]

Of course, such ecstatic sensuousness is hardly unparalleled in devotional writing, even in that of heterosexual men, but it is difficult not to link it to Jacob's own sexuality. His rapturous, agonised voice is that of a Mechtild of Magdeburg, an Angela di Foligno or a Marguerite-Marie Alacoque, as he transposes himself into one of the Holy Women on Calvary, a male-female mourner distraught before the still seductive body of a male-female Christ. More haunted by the Passion than any other French Catholic poet, Jacob commonly casts himself as Veronica wiping her Lord's face on His way to the Cross or, more commonly still, as Mary Magdalene who, after anointing Christ's feet and wiping them with her hair, is the agonised witness of his death on the Cross and then, three days later – afraid, amazed and overjoyed – of His glorious resurrection. More remarkably still, when Cocteau told Jacob of Radiguet's death in December 1923, Jacob tried to console him with the image of Mary at the foot of the Cross: Radiguet as crucified Christ, Cocteau as his lover-cum-mother. Four years later, Jacob wrote to Cocteau of his *amour-admiration* – though much more than mere admiration was involved – for one Louis Vaillant, a young man of Saint-Benoît, describing it as 'genre Madeleine-Christ', like that of Mary Magdalene's for Christ, the same love that Cocteau had felt for Radiguet.[54] At a much lower literary level, Jean Desbordes (another future martyr) fantasises in his mystical-masturbatory farrago *J'adore* about 'the hand of Mary Magdalene who touches men's genitals (*le sexe des hommes*) for their pleasure and the garment of Christ for His light' as he longs for a watery *Liebestod* in which, like an 'ecstatic swimmer', 'Greek lover' or 'dream girl', he would merge with the floodtides of Life.[55] In their different ways, Jacob, Cocteau, Green, Sachs and Desbordes (and also Bourgoint, another devotee of Mary Magdalene and a frequent visitor to her shrine at Saint-Maximin-la-Sainte-Baume near Marseilles) were all seeking – and failing – to marry the Eros and Agape that the institutional Church was committed to keeping rigidly apart. Mary Magdalene may be an unlikely 'gay icon', but her presence, as an embodiment of spirituality and sexuality reconciled and conjoined, in gay French Catholic discourse in the inter-war years, gives an added pungency to the coincidental prominence of the *quartier de la Madeleine* in gay city life at the time, those streets which Poulenc, that 'old tart' (*'vieille putain'*, C p. 917), 'old trollop' (*'vieille grue'*, C p. 955) and 'old scumbag' (*'vieille ordure'*, C p. 715), as he variously styled himself, always considered as his *'village natal'*. And it also helps explain why, of all the churches in Paris, it is to La Madeleine that Genet's Divine always takes her beloved Mignon to Mass, Mignon, that 'earthly expression, [that] symbol of a being (perhaps God), of a heavenly idea',[56] on whose naked chest she fantasises about consecrating the Host, and whose cock, the be-all and end-all of her world, she anoints, impenitent whore that she is, as ardently as Mary Magdalene ever did the feet and head of her Master and Saviour.

Black Virgin: Poulenc at Rocamadour (August 1936)

In the series of interviews Poulenc gave on French radio between October 1953 and April 1954, his interviewer and friend, the music critic Claude Rostand, the originator of the famous *voyou/moine* opposition, encouraged the composer, at the risk of some simplification, to set the 'two faces, apparently perfectly contradictory' of his music in the context of his 'two hereditary sources':

> ... the paternal source from which you derive your sense of gravity and your taste for rigour; the maternal source from which you derive your Parisian, even your *faubourien*, dimension. Whence the two opposed aspects of your music; on the one hand, your personal folklore, aristocratic and popular at one and the same time; and, on the other, the naked, spare lines of certain of your religious works.

'What you want,' Poulenc replied, 'is for me to arrive at a synthesis of what is most paradoxical in my work: the juxtaposition of the profane and the sacred.' (ECR pp. 131-2.) At once seductive and reductive, Rostand's binary conception of his friend's life and work may be expressed and extended as follows:

'FATHER'/'MALE'   'MOTHER'/'FEMALE'

Aveyron   Paris, Nogent
Catholic   secular
sacred   profane
'moine'   *'voyou'*

spirituality/Agape	sexuality/Eros
tradition	modernity
seriousness	*'délicieuse mauvaise musique'*
form	melody, rhythm
orchestra	piano
chorus	solo voice

The final two sets of dyadic pairings are tentative in the extreme, and reflect only the approximate musical tastes of Emile and Jenny Poulenc respectively, plus the all-important fact that it was his mother, 'an exquisite pianist, endowed with an impeccable musical sense and a delightful touch', who introduced Poulenc to the instrument for which he would both compose in abundance and perform on professionally. As with all such sets of binary opposites, it will be necessary partially to deconstruct them as we proceed, but they will provide a valuable framework for a discussion of what was, in more senses than one, the crucial event of Poulenc's life: the encounter with the Black Virgin of Rocamadour in August 1936 and the conversion to Catholicism that ensued.

Following the trauma of Raymonde Linossier's death, Poulenc wrote only an 'Epitaphe', to words by Malherbe, commemorating her death throughout the whole of 1930, and did not resume composition until February 1931. Thereafter he made important progress as a songwriter, setting texts by Apollinaire (1931), Jacob (1932) and, above all, Eluard (1935), these last being premiered by Poulenc and the baritone Pierre Bernac who, more than just the most inspired interpreter, was to be virtually the co-creator of many of his greatest vocal works. In his personal life, Poulenc formed an enduring relationship around this time: his new companion being Raymond Destouches (died 1988), a driver of taxis and ambulances, whom the composer met at Noizay in the early 1930s. Although Destouches was later to marry, and Poulenc to have various other relationships (including at least one with a woman, see the following chapter), the two men remained close and, Poulenc wrote to a *confidente* in 1952 when he was openly associating with another man in Toulon (Lucien Roubert, of whom more in connection with the composition of *Dialogues des Carmélites*), 'although with Raymond there has been what is referred to nowadays as a transference of feeling on my part to something far more paternal, I cannot, after 20 years, cause him any pain, and he will always have first place in my life.' (C p. 740.) Despite the brilliance of much of Poulenc's musical production in the first half of the 1930s, notably of the Concerto for Two Pianos and Orchestra (1932) commissioned by Princesse Edmond de Polignac and the well-known *Suite française* (1935), based on themes by the seventeenth-century composer Claude Gervaise, there is a sense in which it marks time, as though unable to tap the deeper sources of inspiration partially uncovered in *Aubade*. Despite a measure of personal happiness thanks to Raymond Destouches, Poulenc remained in other respects deeply unfulfilled and, some time early in 1936, he embarked upon a Concerto for Organ, String Orchestra and Timpani which was not completed until 1938, and was first performed in June the following year, whence the frequent but erroneous assertion that the work was directly inspired by his 'conversion experience' of August 1936. In fact, as a letter of *May* 1936 to Marie-Blanche de Polignac makes clear, the concerto was begun, and, allegedly, 'almost completed', some months *before* the experience in question. Moreover, it is in the same letter that Poulenc refers to himself living at Noizay like 'a stoutish monk, somewhat dissolute' and to his new work as 'not the amusing Poulenc of the concerto for two pianos but more like a Poulenc en route for the cloister' (C p. 414). Clearly, the familiar concept of *Poulenc le voyou* versus *Poulenc le moine*, the two separated by a datable event in August 1936 cannot be sustained, any more, for example, than the revelation of Christmas Day 1886 marks an absolute dividing line in the life of Claudel.

Poulenc had other reasons for being anxious and depressed in the spring and summer of 1936. In 1931 he had sustained serious losses when the Lyon-Allemand bank crashed, and, for the first time, political events, notably the fascist riots in Paris in February 1934 (see C 392) began, if not to impinge directly on his life, then at least to concern him. Two years later, in May 1936, elections brought to power the anti-fascist Popular Front composed of the three main parties of the political left (Socialists, Radicals, communists) and headed by Léon Blum (1872-1950) who was not only Jewish but known in the Parisian gay milieu to be covertly 'one of us': Poulenc knowingly

POULENC'S HOUSE AT LE GRAND COTEAU AT NOIZAY

called him *'la Léon'*.[57] The coming to power of a communist-backed government, and still more the month of sit-in strikes and mass demonstrations that ensued, threw Poulenc's circle of friends into something like panic, as it did the best part of upper-class Paris, some of whose members began to mutter openly 'better Hitler than Blum'. Sitting in bed under a painting of Saint Philomena at her home on the Place des Etats-Unis, Marie-Laure de Noailles told Jean Hugo of her support for the Front Commun led by Gaston Bergery, a one-time man of the left now far to the right, while Bourgoint, she claimed, was backing the ex-communist Jacques Doriot's Parti Populaire Français, the only large-scale fascist party in France; Sauguet was 'a royalist', Lifar 'on the right', while various other members of her circle were seriously considering emigration. Only Auric was on the left, 'waving his little clenched fist', while Poulenc she described as *'au-dessus de la mêleé'*, above the struggle, though in fact, as we shall see, he was anything but indifferent to the mounting social and political crisis.[58] On 18 July 1936, civil war erupted in Spain, followed by the assassination, shortly afterwards, of Federico García Lorca by which Poulenc was sufficiently moved to dedicate his Violin Sonata of 1943 to the memory of the dead poet; presumably he would have known by then that – yet another sacrificial victim to add to his litany of martyrs – García Lorca was gay. Cursing 'the hard times that make it necessary to play the piano in Carcassonne', Poulenc was continually on the move during the summer of 1936 and it was after spending a miserable ten days at his sister's *château* at Tremblay in Normandy – 'ten days here all alone in a big house, not my own, in the pouring rain – and what rain! – thumping away on a piano that has more fungus than flats' – that, on 15 August, his heart 'full of moss and melancholy', he sent a further letter to Marie-Blanche de Polignac which reveals an unexpected *political* dimension to the personal crisis that, a week later, on 22 August 1936, would bring him face to face with the Black Virgin of Rocamadour.

'Poupoule' begins by telling the Comtesse how much he is 'hating' the year 1936, despite which, and despite continual disruptions, he has been working 'very hard' and has completed, or is close to completing, 'seven beautiful, solemn Chorales [the *Sept chansons* on texts by Apollinaire and Eluard]' and 'a grave and austere Concerto [for Organ]' that 'show a very new trend' in his work, as well as a sequence of piano pieces, *Les Soireés de Nazelles* which mark 'the end of the Biches period – that is, 20 minutes of music for piano *brillantissimo*'. Then, moving on to politics, or, rather to the impact of politics on his own personal fortunes, he begins by '[cursing] Monsieur Blum who terrifies publishers who bury themselves alive in their safes' and then delivers himself of the closest thing to a political credo that he would ever probably make:

> Marie-Blanche, I am not 'Popular Front'. Am I wrong? I am an old French Republican who once believed in liberty. I loathe Monsieur de la Roque, but I used to like Monsieur Loubet well enough. For me, you see, the Republic was men like Clemenceau whose maxim I think of so often: on your feet!!!!! [...] To believe, Marie-Blanche, that I have no left-ish leanings is to know very little about me. I thought I had long ago given proof that popular *fronts* are dear to me and I confess that what pleased me about *Le Quatorze Juillet* [the performance of Romain Rolland's 1902 play of that name with which the Popular Front celebrated its accession to power, with music written for the occasion by, amongst others, Auric, Honegger, Milhaud and Poulenc's former teacher Charles Koechlin] was really the *audience*. All this is very complicated.

> C pp. 419-20, B p. 107

Very complicated indeed: 'Poupoule' is for 'popular *fronts*' but he is not 'Popular Front'. He does not greatly care for 'Monsieur Blum', but makes no comment on the Prime Minister's Jewishness and, in a passage not quoted here, actually compliments the Minister of Education, Jean Zay (1904-44), also a Jew and a future victim of the fascist *milieu*, on his appointing a mutual friend, the playwright Edouard Bourdet, as director of the Comédie Française.[59] He is an old-style Republican who detests Colonel de la Roque (1885-1946) and his ultra-right paramilitary movement, the Croix-de-Feu, and only admires two politicians, both renowned for their anticlericalism and passionate commitment to Dreyfus, Emile Loubet (1838-1929) and Georges Clemenceau (1841-1929); he also preferred the audience at *Le Quatorze Juillet* to the pageant itself, including, it seems, the musical contributions of his friends and associates, which, those of Milhaud and Auric apart, he considered to be 'shit' (C p. 421) – or so he told Henri Sauguet, who had also been sidelined by the new government. In short, with his 'leftish leanings', he is first and foremost a populist and democrat – not exactly what might be expected of a man of his class and connections when old friends of his like Marie-Laure de Noailles were openly admitting ultra-right sympathies and when anti-Semitism – directed not least against his friend and fellow composer Darius Milhaud[60] – reached a level of violence not witnessed since the end of the Dreyfus Affair. To have been politically isolated in this way must have added to Poulenc's habitually melancholic disposition and helped transform the shattering news he received from Hungary, about another young French composer, a couple of days later into a fully-fledged crisis of personal, artistic and metaphysical identity which, in its turn, led directly to the 'conversion experience' of 22 August.

Pierre-Octave Ferroud (1900-36) was not one of Poulenc's closest friends, but as a composer, critic and founder of the chamber music society *Le Triton*, he was an important figure on the French musical scene with whom Poulenc had collaborated on the collective ballet *L'Eventail de Jeanne* of 1929; without being major works, compositions such as *Foules* (1924), *Types* (1931) and the Symphony in A (1930) are crisp, witty exercises in the French modern style in which Poulenc, amongst others, recognised a promising voice of the future.[61] More than most of his French contemporaries, Ferroud was open to the influence of Bartok, and it may have been this that took him to Hungary in the summer of 1936; on 17 August he was killed in a car accident at Debrecen near the Austrian frontier. But it was the manner of his death – decapitation – that seems to have particularly appalled Poulenc when he learned of the tragedy just before leaving Tremblay for a working holiday at Uzerche in the Corrèze. There he joined Bernac and his *répétitrice,* Yvonne Gouverné, who, in an address given at Rocamadour in July 1973 to mark the tenth anniversary of the composer's death, provides the fullest third-person account of his state of mind at the time and of what happened over the next few days:

> I shall always remember Francis Poulenc getting off the train at Uzerche, where Pierre Bernac and I had gone to meet him, in that famous month

THE BLACK VIRGIN OF ROCAMADOUR

of August 1936. 'Ferroud has just been killed in an horrific car accident somewhere near Salzburg,' he said as soon as he saw us. We had spent the previous two summers in Salzburg where we came into daily contact with Pierre-Octave Ferroud – an extremely intelligent musician whose intense musical activities we had often shared. He had founded a chamber music society, Le Triton, for which we gave frequent first performances. Poulenc was deeply affected by his death. The region of Uzerche where we were staying stirred in Francis a sense of his close affinity with Aveyron, birthplace of his father. It was a region conducive to spiritual revelations. Poulenc wanted to go to Rocamadour, an ancient place of pilgrimage which, 30 years ago, did not attract the crowds one finds there today. We all three entered a silent chapel in which stood the statue of the Black Virgin. Outwardly, nothing happened, yet from that moment everything in the spiritual life of Poulenc changed. He bought a little picture with the text of the Litanies to the Black Virgin, and as soon as we were back in Uzerche he began to write that very pure work for female choir and organ, *Les Litanies à la Vierge Noire*.[62]

Like all conversion narratives, including those of Poulenc himself (see below) Gouverné's account dramatises the significance of a single event, and so exaggerates the distinction between a 'before' and an 'after'; in particular, it fails to take into account the clear evidence that, having begun (and possibly almost completed) the Organ Concerto before the events of August 1936, Poulenc had, in his own words, been 'en route for the cloister' for some time before. But August 1936 was, as Poulenc insisted, 'a capital date in my life and career' (ECR p. 108) to which he continually returned, not only in imagination but in fact, revisiting Rocamadour to dedicate to the Virgin at least four of the works – arguably his greatest, along with the original *Litanies à la Vierge Noire* – that he was in the process of composing: *Figure humaine* (written 1943-4), the *Stabat Mater* (1950), *Dialogues des Carmélites* (1953-6) and *Sept répons des Ténèbres* (1960-1). Why, then, did the death of Ferroud focus so shatteringly Poulenc's diffuse, if virtually permanent, sense of melancholy and frustration, and what was it in the encounter with the Black Virgin that released in him hitherto untapped emotional, spiritual and artistic resources?

Rocamadour is about 45 miles south of Uzerche, the other side of Brive-la-
Gaillarde to whose station Poulenc would often come at the start and the
finish of successive pilgrimages to the site. Set vertiginously into a cliff face
overlooking the gorge of the river Alzor, Rocamadour is without question
one of the most extraordinary spectacles in France, and was a major
pilgrimage centre from the early twelfth century until the middle of the
fifteenth, receiving, amongst other notabilities, Saints Bernard, Dominic and
Anthony of Padua (in whose honour Poulenc would compose a set of *Laudes*
in 1957-9), Henry II of England and Simon de Montfort, and a whole
succession of French kings from Saint Louis to Philippe de Valois, whereafter
its celebrity waned until it revived during the Marian renaissance of the mid-
nineteenth century when it was comprehensively restored and reconstructed
under the direction of Monseigneur Bardou, Bishop of Cahors. Its infinitely
evocative name has, unfortunately, nothing to do with doomed lovers casting
themselves off from its rocks, but commemorates the discovery, in 1166, of
the supposed remains of Saint Amadour, traditionally, if somewhat fancifully,
identified with the wealthy but diminutive Zacchaeus – almost a double of
Poulenc – who, in his anxiety to see Jesus, climbs up a sycamore tree and is
greeted and saved by his Lord despite his being the local leader of the detested
publican class (Luke 19: 1-10).[63] By legend the servant of the Virgin Mary
and the husband of Veronica, Saint Amadour was also believed to have carved
the black wooden statuette of the Madonna and Child which was, and
remains, the principal focus of the tens of thousands of pilgrims and tourists
who visit the site. Notre-Dame de Rocamadour is one of the 40 or so
surviving Black Virgins in France, out of an estimated total of 190 at the
outbreak of the wars of religion in 1561. Many were destroyed at that time
by Protestant iconoclasts, and others still 'perished' at the hands of
revolutionary vandals in the 1790s, so that, of those that survive, not a few
are seventeenth- and even nineteenth-century copies; though almost certainly
not the original figure on the site, the existing Notre-Dame de Rocamadour
probably dates from the thirteenth century. By far the largest concentration of
surviving Black Virgins is in or around the Massif Central, the Poulencs' (as
opposed to the Royers') ancestral terrain, and even beside such memorable
figures as Notre-Dame de Marsat (Puy-de-Dôme), Notre-Dame de la
Négrette (Espalian, Aveyron), Notre-Dame des Neiges (Aurillac, Cantal) and

the extraordinary turbanned Notre-Dame de Meymac in the Corrèze, Notre-Dame de Rocamadour has a magic and mana all of her own, either as a bare emaciated black figure with a diminutive, but clearly adult, Christ on her knee or clothed in her ceremonial vestments on Marian feast-days. Her magnetism is heightened by her location in a tiny crypt-like chapel carved out of the rock and reached by a stone staircase, at each of whose 223 steps pilgrims were required to kneel and pray in order to receive the *sportelle* or *senhal* in Provençal, a lead medallion of the virgin that 'purchased' the appropriate number of indulgences for sins. For sheer concentrated charisma, Notre-Dame de Rocamadour's only rivals are the Black Virgins of Montserrat near Barcelona and the Jasna Góra monastery at Czestochowa in Poland.

But why are she and her sister-images black? The idea that the Black Virgins' *négritude* is an accidental consequence of centuries of candle smoke is rejected by all writers on the subject. Black Virgins are either made of naturally black wood or stone or are deliberately painted black; their blackness is integral to their meaning. All, too, are tiny – at 69 centimetres, Notre-Dame de Rocamadour is in fact one of the tallest – and all are majestic, hieratic and almost expressionless, devoid, at any rate, of the smiles, tears and looks of tenderness and compassion that characterise the standard 'White Virgins' of Catholic Christianity: they are perhaps the least 'human' images of the Mother of God in existence. All, or nearly all, are said by legend to come from, or to be linked to, 'the East', and many have arrived miraculously, by sea or by air, at their present locations; all are credited with supernatural powers of healing and/or converting those who approach them with the proper humility. Studies of the Black Virgin usually link her blackness to the Shulamite woman of the 'Song of Songs' who, in her turn, figures as a 'type' or Old Testament model for the Virgin Mary of the New: *Nigra sum sed formosa filiae Jerusalem sicut tabernacula Cedar, sicut pelles Salomonis* (I am black, but comely, O ye daughters of Jerusalem, as the tents of Kedar, as the curtains of Solomon, Song of Songs 1: 5). A link is also sometimes made to the 'overshadowing' of the Virgin by the Holy Spirit at the moment of the conception of Jesus (Luke 1: 35); the Virgin is black because she is fertile, ready for 'insemination' by the Spirit of the Most High. But, although the Black Virgin is a thoroughly Christian (or Christianised) image, behind and

POULENC WITH YVONNE GOUVERNÉ AT UZERCHE IN AUGUST 1936,
SHORTLY AFTER HIS VISIT TO ROCAMADOUR

beneath her lie other Mother Goddesses, denizens of 'the East' to which she is so commonly linked: Greco-Roman Cybele, Syrian Astarté, Phoenician-Carthaginian Tanith and, above all, Egyptian Isis – not for nothing was the celebrated Notre-Dame du Puy known as *'L'Egyptienne'*. 'It is with Isis that the image of the Mother of God presents the greatest resemblance', writes the leading expert on the origins of the Black Virgin, quoting the Goddess' celebrated announcement of herself in the closing pages of Apuleius' *Metamorphoses*, better known as The Golden Ass (second century, CE):

> I am Nature, the universal Mother, mistress of all the elements, primordial child of time, sovereign of all things spiritual, queen of the dead, queen also of the immortals, the single manifestation of all gods and goddesses that are. Though I am worshipped in many aspects, known by countless names, and propitiated with all manner of different ties, yet the whole round earth venerates me. The primeval Phrygians call me Pessinuntica, Mother of the gods; the Athenians, sprung from their own soil, call me Cecropian Artemis; for the islanders of Cyprus I am Paphian Aphrodite; for the archers of Crete I am Dictynna; for the trilingual Sicilians, Stygian Proserpine; and for the Eleusinians their ancient Mother of the Corn. I have come in pity of your plight, I have come to favour and aid you. Weep no more, lament no longer; the hour of deliverance, shone over by my watchful light, is at hand.[64]

When, therefore, Poulenc ascended the steps to the Black Virgin's chapel, teetering on 'a vertiginous anfractuosity of rock', indeed 'half constructed in the rock' (ECR p. 108), he came, did he but know it, as a neophyte, burdened with grief and frustration, in quest of personal and creative renewal. Entering, he came face to face with a diminutive statue that concentrated into itself all the mysterious and contradictory energies of the Anima or Great Mother. Born of the black earth, reaching back beyond Christianity into the 'dark backward and abysm of time', bearing within her both life and death, fertility and destruction, but also pointing upwards and outwards to spiritual enlightenment, Notre-Dame de Rocamadour offered, for one in Poulenc's predicament, a possibility of metamorphosis at the price of dying as one self and being reborn as another. In addition, as Benjamin Ivry has well noted, there is an 'uncanny resemblance' between the statue with its 'thick lips, heavy eyebrows, a beak-like nose and high cheekbones' and Poulenc's personal anima, the late Raymonde Linossier, a 'coincidence' that, someone as 'visually orientated' as was Poulenc, is unlikely to have missed.[65] Individual and collective archetypes met in a single dark figure, remote, other worldly yet compassionate withal: the kind of sacred presence, *fascinans et tremendum* to whom or to which one can only say *'Vous'*. Yet, paradoxically, what, in biographical, psychological and musical terms, Poulenc was initiated into by the discovery of the Black Virgin was *not* the world of his Parisian mother – that world of secular happiness, lyricism and high spirits on which he had drawn, perhaps *ad satietatem*, for most of the music he had written up to then – but the repressed religious world of his Auvergnat father, serious and substantial, on which he had almost deliberately turned his back when he was swept into the social and artistic whirl of Le Boeuf sur le Toit. The Black Virgin delivered Poulenc into the hands of his Father and, literally overnight, his work took on a greater resonance and density.

Amongst the miracles attributed to Notre-Dame de Rocamadour is that of restoring speech to the dumb and, though Poulenc in 1936 was in no way suffering from the composer's equivalent of 'writer's block', it is nonetheless remarkable that, on his own account, the opening lines of his *Litanies à la Vierge Noire* 'came' to him on the very evening that he returned to Uzerche from what had begun as a simple day-trip to a well-known site of pilgrimage. The *Litanies* are a setting for women's or children's voices and organ of a devotional text he picked up at Rocamadour, and he was adamant that this, his first religious work, should be sung with what he called 'peasant devoutness' in keeping with the rough-hewn, unsophisticated nature of the place and figure that inspired it (ECR p. 109). Writing to Nadia Boulanger shortly after beginning the work, Poulenc stated that, in it, 'the Aveyron half of my blood suddenly and roughly triumphs over my Nogentais half. What's more I am clinging wildly to this richer and more austere blood which "ought" to permit me to grow old gracefully.' (C p. 428.) The key words here are 'suddenly' and 'roughly' (*'âprement'*): thanks to the intervention of a force that Poulenc clearly believed to be of supernatural origin (his new piece, he told fellow composer Henri Sauguet, convinced him that there are 'gifts that come to us from above *(de l'au-delà)*' (C p. 427)). He and his music have been abruptly deflected from their former 'maternal' focus, sophisticated and urbane to the point of slickness, and are reconfiguring themselves around the rediscovered 'paternal' axis, robust, rudimentary and rich in energy and potential. It is a Virgin – not the White Virgin of the *élite* but the Black Virgin of the peasantry – who admits him to the Father before whom he, in his turn, becomes as a woman or child, begging forgiveness and seeking renewal in music of a plangency that even he would never equal:

> *Reine, à qui Roland consacra son épée,*
> *priez pour nous.*
> *Reine, dont la bannière gagna les batailles,*
> *priez pour nous.*
> *Reine, dont la main délivrait les captifs,*
> *priez pour nous.*
> *Notre-Dame, dont le pèlerinage est enrichi de faveurs spéciales,*
> *Notre-Dame, que l'impiété et la haine ont voulu souvent détruire,*
> *Notre-Dame, que les peuples visitent comme autrefois,*
> *Priez pour nous, priez pour nous.*[66]

[Queen, to whom Roland consecrated his sword,/pray for us./Queen, whose flag won battles,/pray for us./Queen, whose hand freed prisoners,/pray for us./Our Lady, whose pilgrimage is enriched with special favours,/Our Lady, whom impiety and hate have often sought to destroy,/Our Lady, whom the nations visit now as yesterday,/Pray for us, pray for us.]

Poulenc's 'conversion', like virtually every other such psychological-spiritual transformation, was not a once-and-for-all event but a *process*: it had been in incubation, so to speak, since the spring of 1936 (or even since the great crisis of 1928-30) and would require several years before it took on doctrinal shape. In psychological and artistic terms, what changed was the predominantly matrifocal nature of Poulenc's life and work hitherto: the Great Mother showed him the way to the Father and, in so doing, added a 'masculine' strength and austerity to the 'feminine' sparkle and grace of the bulk of the music he had written to date. Henceforth, his work would possess what Cocteau called 'the supernatural [i.e. double] sex of beauty', 'contour' ('masculine') as well as charm ('feminine'), intensity and rigour as well as elegant high spirits.[67] 'Art', according to Cocteau is, 'born of the copulation (*coït*) between the male element and the female element of which all of us are composed and which are better balanced (*plus équilibrés*) in the artist than in other men (*sic*).'[68] What happened to Poulenc in and after August 1936 was that, artistically, he achieved a kind of ambisexual equilibrium that would allow him at last to give birth to the semi-formed works that lay dormant within him, locked in what he, several times, calls the *'limbes'* ('limbo') of his creative imagination (see C pp. 68, 71, 348); not for nothing were Black Virgins credited with the power of giving life to the stillborn. More and more, Poulenc came to speak of artistic creation as a process of birthing and of the newborn works as his 'children' (see C pp. 643, 645, 692, etc.), as though he, like the Black Virgin, had been 'over-shadowed' by the artistic equivalent of the Holy Spirit which enabled him to bring forth his musical offspring, as it were, parthenogenetically.[69] The analogy between music and child is strikingly foregrounded in the summer of 1946 (see C pp. 628, 629) just before the birth of Poulenc's own love child, Marie-Ange (13 September 1946), the child whom, unlike his music, he would never publicly acknowledge but whom privately he considered his own. Artistically, Poulenc is mother-and-father in one, both fertilised and fertilising, so that if he is 'delivered with neither pain nor anaesthetics' (*'accouché sans aucune douleur et sans anesthésie'*, (C p. 846)) of the song cycle *Le Travail du peintre* (1957), it is also he who 'impregnates' Denise Duval in such a way that she becomes the co-creatrix of the 'beautiful sad child' (*'bel enfant triste'*) that is *La Voix humaine* in whose 'gestation' she has played so important a role: 'With us, it's as though we were making children together (*nous c'est comme si on faisait des enfants ensemble*). No-one has fecundated you more than me!!! Who would have believed it?' (C p. 935.) Double-gendered,[70] Poulenc would henceforth be, as he put it, *'plein de musique'* (C pp. 497, 498, 499), not just 'full of music' but 'pregnant with music', and the traumatic period that he, France and Europe were about to enter would not so much impede as stimulate his new-found creative fertility. Suffering, both individual and collective, would become not just the overt theme of much of his work, but would gradually emerge as the precondition of artistic creativity, the very matrix of the best of the music he would compose in the future.

Faith, death and freedom:
Poulenc's music 1937-50

'Whatever its etymology,' Wilfred Mellers has well written, 'the name Rocamadour hints at rock, hardness, bitterness *and* love.'[71] All of these elements would be present in the music that Poulenc composed between the 'conversion experience' of August 1936 and the outbreak of war three years later. Much of it was written at Anost, near Autun in the Morvan, amidst a rugged landscape similar to, if less spectacular than, Rocamadour, which Poulenc explicitly identified with his Auvergnat father. He kept a photograph of Autun cathedral on his mantelpiece 'as others have of a beloved woman' (C p. 555) and was similarly drawn to craggy cathedrals and churches such as those of Vézélay (another shrine to Mary Magdalene), Moissac, Conques and Le Puy (also home to a famous Black Virgin) which, like Notre-Dame de Rocamadour, seem to be hewn from the very substance of the land from which they emerge; Poulenc's religious sensibility, and the music he wrote to express it, was emphatically more Romanesque than Gothic.[72] It was at Anost in the summer of 1937 that Poulenc wrote his Mass in G, dedicated to the memory of his father, his first large-scale liturgical work which, in omitting the Credo (a sign, perhaps, both of continuing spiritual and musical uncertainty), throws the emphasis on the twin pillars of Poulenc's Catholicism: praise (the Gloria) and contrition (the Kyrie and Agnus Dei). But Poulenc's music of 1937-9 is not informed by any sudden influx of spiritual and emotional peace. On the contrary, its most characteristic mood is *aridity*, captured to perfection in a little-performed work of 1937, *Sécheresses*, commissioned by the wealthy English dilettante and collector, Edward James (1907-84), to a set of prose poems he had published, with illustrations by Dalí, in the review *Minotaure*; an occasional visitor to Noizay, James was an overt and active homosexual. *Sécheresses* was not well received, either on its first performance in May 1938 or on its rare reappearances subsequently, and is usually written off as a 'transitional' work that produced no worthwhile musical progeny. Poulenc, however, rated it highly, and, as Mellers says, it is a 'score of unwanted ferocity, in its aggressive pattern-making and harsh, Stravinskian scoring', 'the exact musical analogue of the texts' Dalí- and Tanguy-like images of skeletons, pulverised deserts, and waste lands [which] chimed with [Poulenc's] mood in the wake of Ferroud's death, as well as with Europe's pre-war malaise'.[73] Divided into four sections ('Grasshoppers', 'The Abandoned Village', 'The False Future', 'The Skeleton of the Sea'), the piece reaches what Poulenc himself called a climax of 'anxiety (of anguish, to be more precise)' (C p. 462) in the final movement, above all with the words, *'J'ai attendu trop longtemps la vie qui ne vient pas, la vie de l'autre que je n'ai pas trouvé'* ('For too long I have waited for life that does not come, the life of the other that I have not found'), that spoke all too pertinently of his own continuing aridity amidst the worsening European situation. Private and public anguish are likewise present in the great Concerto for Organ, Strings and Timpani, begun before the 'conversion experience' of 1936 but, it is reasonable to assume, substantially reworked between then and its first performance in June 1939. Replete with 'wars and rumours of war' (Matthew 24: 6), the Concerto, like Vaughan Williams' Fourth Symphony (1935), has been read retrospectively as prophetic of the catastrophes to come, but its alternating turmoil and astringency are as much about present inner conflict as harbingers of imminent historical upheaval. Poulenc may have been, as he said, 'en route for the cloister' when he began it, but, having metaphorically entered that cloister after August 1936, it is anything but peace that he has found there.

Rocamadour 1936 may be the crucial turning point in Poulenc's life and work, but the rediscovery of Paul Eluard – whom Poulenc had met in 1917, but not seen since – in 1935 was to be of scarcely less importance for the future of his music. The distance between Poulenc's initial set of five poems by Eluard, written in March 1935, and the song cycle *Tel jour telle nuit*, written in December 1936 and January 1937, is immense, and can only be attributed to the extraordinary enrichment of the composer's whole universe consequent upon the 'conversion experience' of August 1936. In *Cinq poèmes de Paul Eluard*, Poulenc, in Bernac's view, 'had not yet found his own

Eluardian lyricism'; each song is a separate entity, unrelated musically or thematically to its fellows, unlike *Tel jour telle nuit* which, in conscious imitation of Schumann's *Dichterliebe* (1840) or Fauré's *La Bonne Chanson* (1894), was conceived from the outset as an integrated cycle of nine poems, arranged in such a way as to suggest both a musical and a psychological progression in keeping with the new purposiveness that had entered Poulenc's life and work in the aftermath of Rocamadour. With the exception of the final poem 'Nous avons fait la nuit' (from *Facile* (1935)), all the texts of *Tel jour telle nuit* came from Eluard's most recent collection *Les Yeux fertiles* (1936); the overall title was supplied by Eluard, though the choice of texts – by no means an obvious selection, given the range and complexity of the poet's themes – was Poulenc's own. Like the *Litanies*, the songs of *Tel jour telle nuit* often have their origins in chance encounters and connections which seem almost instantly to have generated the appropriate musical form. Thus, a Sunday afternoon stroll near the Place de la Bastille in the east of Paris in November 1936 caused Poulenc to recite to himself the poem 'Bonne journée' (dedicated by Eluard to Picasso, and inspired by the former's stay in Spain between January and May 1936 in connection with the first Picasso retrospective in his native country), and 'that evening the music came of itself' and gave the cycle its unforgettable beginning. Song four, 'Une roulotte couverte en tuiles' ('A Gypsy Caravan with a Roof of Tiles') 'came' to Poulenc after seeing a boy 'resembling' the gypsy child of the poem 'on a late November afternoon at Ménilmontant' (always the working-class east of Paris, never the bourgeois west), while the exquisite sixth song, 'Une herbe pauvre' ('Scanty Grass'), the fulcrum of the whole cycle inspired by the sight of the first blade of grass in a snowbound landscape, reminded Poulenc of the 'invigorating bitterness of a flower I once plucked and tasted in the surroundings of the Grande Chartreuse': once again the bleak, craggy landscape that was so often the source of Poulenc's finest inspirations.[74] But it is the final song, 'Nous avons fait la nuit' ('We Have Made Night', meaning 'we have turned out the light'), that marks the real psychological and musical breakthrough and, as Bernac says, attains a level of lyricism 'which is scarcely equalled in the vocal literature of the twentieth century'. A couple lie in bed, the man reflects upon the woman's many qualities and, as they both drift into sleep, feels his partner detach herself from him and become her essential self:

Et dans ma tête qui se met doucement
D'accord avec la tienne avec la nuit
Je m'émerveille de l'inconnue que tu deviens
Une inconnue semblable à toi semblable à tout ce que j'aime
Qui est toujours nouveau.

[And in my head which gently begins/To harmonise with yours with the night/I marvel at the stranger that you become/A stranger resembling you resembling all that I love/Which is ever new.]

It is one of the key revelations of the 'Thou-ness' of the beloved, of the discovery of his or her otherness-and-sameness and of the with-ness that unites the lovers over and above their separateness, and it draws appropriately passionate and affirmative music from the composer. 'I wrote this song in the sincerest of emotions,' Poulenc would later write in his Journal de mes mélodies (1964), 'I hope others can sense it. The piano coda is essential. It is difficult to convince performers that *only calm* can give intensity to a poem about love. Everything else is superfluous (*Tout le reste est baisers de nourrice)*.' (J p. 22.)

By the time *Tel jour telle nuit* was first performed in February 1937, Eluard was closely and publicly associated with the cause of Spanish republicanism and with the anti-fascist struggle as a whole, and his political stance, both then and later, would exercise a powerful influence over Poulenc. It did not make Poulenc a man of the Left, or transform his work into some kind of *musique engagée*, but it did turn him decisively away from the rightist, and later collaborationist, path that so many of his social equals would espouse; Eluard's fundamental optimism also helped preserve him from the underlying depressive streak in his character. Between 1938 and 1944, almost all of Poulenc's work would relate directly or contrapuntally to the experience of war, defeat, resistance and liberation, and Eluard's influence must be considered vital in leading Poulenc, in the poet's famous words, *'de l'horizon d'un homme à l'horizon de tous'* ('from the horizon of one man to the horizon of all'). The Munich crisis of September 1938 inspired the exquisite setting of 'Priez pour paix' by Charles d'Orléans (1394-1465), a further and still more urgent invocation of the Virgin's intercession in the cause of peace. Poulenc found the text in *Le Figaro* on the morning of 28 September, the day before the 'conference' opened, and set it to music immediately: 'I tried to give here a feeling of fervour and above all of humility (for me the most beautiful quality of prayer),' he wrote. 'It is a prayer for a country church. My conception of religious music is essentially direct and often intimate.' (J pp. 27-8.) Directness and intimacy – which is not to say simplicity – are also the outstanding qualities of Poulenc's last peacetime composition, the extraordinarily bleak and anguished *Quatre motets pour un temps de pénitence*, written between July 1938 and January 1939, in which, inspired by the example of Tomás Luiz de Victoria (c.1550-1611) – 'the Saint John of the Cross of music' (ECR p. 157) – Poulenc entered, for the first but certainly not for the last time, the sacred Christian space par excellence, Gethsamene and Golgotha, there to commemorate in awe the ultimate mystery of the abandonment of God by God and, following upon the saving sacrifice of Christ, grimly to foreshadow the terrible sacrifices about to happen. Shortly after the outbreak of hostilities, Poulenc wrote another masterpiece of controlled pathos, his setting of Guillaume Apollinaire's 1917 poem 'Bleuet' (literally 'Cornflower', *un bleu* being a First World War colloquialism for a raw recruit) in which memories of Ferroud's violent and untimely death surely mingle with horror at the imminent sacrifice of further youthful lives:

Il est dix-sept heures
Et tu saurais mourir
Si non mieux que tes aînés
Du moins plus pieusement
Car tu connais mieux la mort que la vie

[It is five in the afternoon/And you should know how to die/If not better than your elders/At least more piously/For you know death better than life]

The lifeless human body also provides the central theme of two of the five songs (*Fiançailles pour rire*) that Poulenc composed in September and October 1939 on texts by his friend Louise de Vilmorin (1902-69), the future partner of André Malraux, who was at that time beleaguered in her then husband's castle in Hungary: 'Dans l'herbe' ('He died alone in the woods/beneath the tree of his childhood') and 'Mon cadavre est doux comme un gant' ('My Corpse is as Limp as a Glove'). More and more, the image of the (male) corpse was establishing itself as a key motif in Poulenc's music.

Poulenc was belatedly called up in June 1940, and was in Cahors, and then Brive, as France collapsed about him, the armistice was signed, and the ordeal of occupation and collaboration began. Like not a few French artists and intellectuals, Poulenc felt curiously relieved, even elated, by the experience of defeat, and the sense of a strangely relaxing *far niente* that ensued. 'In a word, I am *happy*. *Yes, I am*,' he wrote to Bernac from Cahors on 10 July, the day the Assembleé Nationale convened in Vichy voted the Third Republic out of existence: 'Divine food, exquisite Cahors wine.' (C p. 498.) It is this utterly ambiguous mood that Poulenc captures in two remarkable compositions of the second half of 1940, the brief piano piece *Mélancolie* (June–August 1940), wistful and detached, utterly unlike those other masterworks of the defeat, Honegger's Symphony No. 2 for String Orchestra and Trumpet (1941) and Messiaen's *Quartet for the End of Time*, written in Stalag 8A at Görlitz in Silesia in 1940, each replete with explicit apocalyptic references, and the setting of five poems by Apollinaire (*Banalités*, October–November 1940), of which the second, entitled 'Hôtel', is a minor masterpiece of nonchalant despair:

> Ma chambre a la forme d'une cage
> Le soleil passe son bras par la fenêtre
> Mais moi qui veux fumer pour faire des mirages
> J'allume au feu du jour ma cigarette
> Je ne veux pas travailler je veux fumer

[My room has the form of a cage/ The sun puts its arms through the window/ But I who want to smoke to create mirages/ I light my cigarette by daylight's flame/ I don't want to work I want to smoke]

Poulenc's letters from Cahors in July 1940 may suggest to some a Pétainist in the making, with their fulsome gratitude to 'the dear Maréchal' for saving him and his unit and enthusiasm for the peasants amongst whom he found himself (C pp. 498-9). His 1942 settings of the *Chansons villageoises* by the Tourangeau poet, Maurice Fombeure (1906-81), might be seen as a musical version of the Vichyist *retour à la terre*, but to claim, as Bernard Ivry does, that the 1942 ballet *Les Animaux modèles*, based on fables by La Fontaine, is 'a Pétainist work' because it allegedly 'abides by' the regime's idealisation of rural life is absurd, especially when its penultimate number – a cockfight – includes a bellicose anti-German song of yesteryear, 'Non, non, vous n'aurez pas notre Alsace-Lorraine', to the conspiratorial delight of those in the audience who recognised it. Though Poulenc was in no sense an active resister, or even a resister by abstention (as was Bernac, who refused to perform on French radio), he did not, in Isaiah Berlin's singularly apt phrase, 'cosy up' to the German occupiers and their Vichyist allies in the manner of so many in his artistic and social milieu: people like Coco Chanel and Serge Lifar, who choreographed *Les Animaux modèles* and who, after the liberation, Poulenc regarded as having been 'childishly imprudent out of his fondness for publicity' (C p. 578). Nor did he give any support to schemes designed to promote Franco-German 'cultural understanding' as did Honegger, inadvertently, when he went to Vienna in 1941 for the 150th anniversary of Mozart's death or, far more culpably, as did Cocteau in befriending and championing the German sculptor Arno Brecker, whose colossal muscle-bound male nudes – practically Tom of Finlands in marble – epitomised the kitsch pseudo-classicism of Nazi aesthetics; 'if these statues ever have erections,' the dramatist Sacha Guitry (another notorious 'cosier-up' to the Germans) told Cocteau at the Brecker exhibition at the Orangerie in 1942, ' we won't be able to move.'[75]

Much controversy has been generated by the role of homosexuals under Vichy in particular and, more generally, in occupied France as a whole. Although the age of consent for homosexual acts was raised by the regime to 21 in August 1942, a significant number of Vichy activists were homosexuals, especially in the educational and cultural fields.[76] Two of the regime's ministers of education, Abel Bonnard and Jérôme Carcopino, were gay, the latter – though he did his best to conceal it – the brother of the novelist and poet Francis Carco (1886-1958) whose *Jésus-la-Caille* (1914) was one of the first novels to speak openly of Parisian homosexuality at street level. The novelist and journalist Robert Brasillach (1909-45) was the most publicly visible member of the so-called *'Gestapette'* (*'tapette'*=queer) of pro-Nazi French homosexual writers and was executed during the *épuration*, and a number of other gay writers (Montherlant, Jouhandeau) endorsed one or another aspect of Vichyist ideology or values, thus giving some plausibility to the figure of the homosexual collaborator, Daniel, in Sartre's *Les Chemins de la liberté* (1945-9). But Poulenc's wartime musical output is, of itself, enough to put paid to any lingering notion of a necessary connection between homosexuality and collaboration. In 1943 Poulenc set to music two poems by the communist 'poet laureate' Louis Aragon: the heart-rending 'C', each line of which rhymes with (*les ponts de*) Cé, the sequence of bridges over the Loire near Angers, the crossing of which figures the defeat and dismemberment of France in 1940, and the mordant 'Fêtes galantes' with its disarmingly offhand depiction of life in occupied Paris:

> *On voit des marquis sur des bicyclettes*
> *On voit des marlous en cheval jupon*
> *On voit des morveux avec des voilettes*
> *On voit des pompiers brûler les pompons [...]*
>
> *On voit chômer les marchands de chaussures*
> *On voit mourir d'ennui les mireurs d'œufs*
> *On voit péricliter les valeurs sûres*
> *Et fuire la vie à la six quatre deux.*

[You see fops on bicycles/you see pimps in kilts/you see brats with veils/ you see firemen burning their pompons [...]/you see out-of-work shoemakers/you see egg candlers bored to death/you see true values in jeopardy/and life whirling by in a slapdash way.][77]

It was, however, his stunning large-scale choral work, *Figure humaine*, based on texts by Eluard and composed at Beaulieu-sur-Dordogne in the Corrèze – the Poulenc heartland again – in the summer of 1943 that retrospectively established Poulenc's reputation as *the* musical voice of the Resistance – retrospectively, because, unable, for obvious reasons, to be publicly performed in occupied France, it was not premiered until January 1945, and even then in London, and in English translation, with Poulenc having been flown in by special military plane to attend the final rehearsals; surprisingly, there was no Paris performance until May 1947.[78] Of the composition's eight parts, it is the last one, 'Liberté', that subsumes and finally dominates the whole cantata, not surprisingly since Eluard's text, so eloquent in its evocation and praise of freedom that hundreds of thousands of copies of it were dropped by allied aircraft over occupied France, is without doubt the most widely read and best-loved poem in twentieth-century French literature. Poulenc discovered it in 1942 when he received his typewritten copy of Eluard's *Poésie et vérité 1942* that was passed hand to hand amongst networks of friends and, as was his wont, almost instantly found the musical form appropriate to the test:

> I wrote *Figure humaine* in a semi-religious mood, anyway. In 1943 so many people had just been imprisoned then deported and even shot, and you can imagine what it meant to me to see these grey-green uniforms marching through Paris. Finding in Eluard's poems the exact equivalent of what I felt, I set to work with complete faith, not without having commended my labours to Our Lady of Rocamadour.

'Liberté' is, as Poulenc says, 'a genuine litany', — consisting of twenty four-line stanzas each concluding with the words *'J'écris ton nom'*, as of a lover carving his beloved's name on a tree, with the three preceding lines, almost all beginning with the word *'sur'*, assembling objects and experiences evocative of freedom, a spool of images rendered even more hypnotic by Poulenc's hushed setting for double chorus. Typical is the following stanza, surely the best four-line evocation of a dog in literature:

> *Sur mon chien gourmand et tendre*
> *Sur ses oreilles dressées*
> *Sur sa patte maladroite*
> *J'écris ton nom*

[On my greedy tender dog/On his pricked up ears/On his clumsy paw/I write your name]

Without freedom, it is implied, even the experience of stroking a dog's ears or taking its clumsily offered paw is vitiated, devalued. Finally, in a crescendo of exaltation, the double choir proclaims the meaning of the litany:

Et par le pouvoir d'un mot
Je recommence ma vie
Je suis né pour to connaître
Pour te nommer
Liberté

[And through the power of a word/I begin my life anew/I was born to know you/To name you Liberty]

Poulenc was justly proud of *Figure humaine*, playing 'Liberté' to himself on the piano every day prior to the Liberation, and, when Paris was liberated, placing the manuscript of the score in the window of his apartment as a sign that he too 'had done his bit'. The works brings together, as no other does, the Catholic and the humanist in Poulenc in a single 'act of faith' (ECR p. 103) and its music transcends any straightforward opposition between the 'sacred' and the 'secular'. Eluard, to whom, as to Bernac, Poulenc owed so much, entitled one of his finest post-war collections *Poésie ininterrompue* (1946); since the breakthrough of August 1936, Poulenc's output, too, had consisted on *musique ininterrompue* that had taken him from self-enclosed misery and frustration to a truly Catholic openness towards the world and other people. '*J'avoue ma vie j'avoue ma mort j'avoue autrui*' ('I acknowledge my life I acknowledge my death I acknowledge others'): this line of Eluard, which Poulenc set to music in his beautiful cantata, *Un soir de neige*, written over Christmas 1944 on the theme of liberated but still cold and hungry Paris, resumes his whole spiritual and moral trajectory since Ferroud's death and the encounter with the Virgin.

Poulenc's new-found universalism did not so much exclude as require the comic, and, to the horror of some critics, he began to write his *opéra-bouffe*, *Les Mamelles de Tirésias* (first performed June 1947), at the very time, May 1944, that the struggle for France and Europe entered its climacteric: 'I had always believed I would write *Les Mamelles* during a happy summer. It has,

alas, been nothing of the sort.' (C p. 553.) *Les Mamelles* sets to music
Apollinaire's 'surreal drama' of that title, the first performance of which
Poulenc had attended as an 18-year-old in 1917. The opera marks a return to
the Pythonesque territory of *Les Mariés de la Tour Eiffel* – the Python, now, of
'Every Sperm is Sacred', for its theme is the government-imposed obligation
of all subjects of the decidedly nebulous polity of 'Zanzibar' to produce
children in abundance for the service of the state. In the wake of the Vichyist
obsession with French *dénatalité* (*'trop peu d'enfants'* was Pétain's reply when
asked to explain the defeat of 1940), both play and opera have an offbeat
topicality and, in addition, a wholly unexpected link with Poulenc's personal
life: on 13 September 1946, he became, as we have seen, the father of a
daughter, Marie-Ange, the fruit of a relationship with a distant relative of his
long-time friend, the art dealer Richard Chanlaire. Poulenc's bisexuality and
unscheduled paternity give an extra piquancy to the opera's themes of
reproduction and 'gender bending'. In the face of the state's frenetic natalist
injunctions, its heroine, the 'feminist' Thérèse, decides to abjure husband and
gender and, literally casting her breasts (in the form of coloured balloons) to
the wind, vows that she will become a soldier, an advocate, a deputy, a
senator, a mathematician, a busboy in a restaurant, anything rather than
produce children for her doltish husband and the virtual police state of
'Zanzibar'. Her resolution instantly endows her with moustache and beard,
and she promptly assumes a name appropriate to her new condition as *un
homme-madame*: Tirésias. For his part, her unnamed husband is unexpectedly
blessed with the capacity to produce children *ad libitum* without the assistance
of a woman (a comprehensive subversion and inversion of the doctrine of the
virgin birth) and, a *fille-père* endowed with a quite prodigious 'maternalised
paternal instinct' (*'instinct paternel maternisé'*), spawns no fewer than 40,049
children on the first day alone of his transformation. We need not follow the
zany plot (at the end of which 'proper' gender roles are of course restored) to
realise that Thérèse-Tirésias and, still more, her parthenogenetic husband
resolve, in absurdist mode, at least the sexual dualities of 'Poulenc-Janus'.[79]
But the deeper problem of his doubleness continued unresolved – he was, he
said, 'as pied as a horse' when it came to his faith, 'not totally impious' but
not nearly 'as religious as I would like to be' (C p. 714) and would come to
the fore when he returned to composing religious music after the war.

Poulenc wrote little actual religious music during the occupation and for some years after (an 'Exultate Deo' and 'Salve Regina', both in May 1941), and it was not until the summer of 1948 that Poulenc-*moine* returned to the scene with *Quatre petites prières de Saint Francis d'Assise*, dedicated to 'the *Frères mineurs* of Champfleury, and especially to Brother Jérôme in memory of his grandfather: my uncle Camille Poulenc'. It is an intimate, miniaturist work, which deliberately eschews the great Franciscan hymns to Brother Sun and Sister Wind, and points forward to the equally benign and affecting *Quatre motets pour un temps de Noël* (1952), written, Poulenc said, as 'a counterpart to the austere *Pénitences*' of 1939. In between came a far more substantial work, the *Stabat Mater*, written in the summer of 1950 and first performed in June 1951, inspired by the death and dedicated to the memory of the gay artist and stage designer, Christian Bérard, who had died, aged only 47, in 1949. Poulenc had originally intended to write a requiem for his late friend but, as so often before, found it was only by projecting himself into female persona – here the grieving Virgin at the foot of the Cross – that he could express his feelings to the full. Once he had thus 'feminised' himself, the writing, not for the first time, came so easily to him that he was 'back in the time of the Mass at Anost' and believed that there must be 'a Rocamadour miracle behind it', not inappropriately since the soul of 'Bébé' Bérard was being musically entrusted to the care of the Black Virgin. But the Stabat is very different from the 'romanesque' religious works that Poulenc had written in the Morvan (it itself was entirely composed at Noizay) and, realising this, Poulenc compared it to the 'Jesuit style' of the Parisian parish churches of Saint-Eustache and Saint-Roch (ECR p. 111). And here, perhaps, lies the problem. The *Stabat* is, given Poulenc's own set of binary oppositions, almost a contradiction in terms: a *Parisian* religious work, written in the grand style for soprano soloist, mixed chorus and orchestra, and, some will find, overblown, even glib, when compared to the concentrated, almost self-effacing, 'romanesque' masterpieces of the past. It is probably the least moving of all Poulenc's sacred compositions, and though he followed it with a typically exquisite (and explicitly 'romanesque') 'Ave Verum Corpus' in 1952, the feeling remains that the rich vein of spirituality made available to him by the 'Rocamadour experience' of August 1936 was now close to exhaustion. Having produced work after work with something of the prolificity of the super-fertile *fille-père* in *Les Mamelles de Tirésias*, Poulenc was approaching a new crisis in his life and music, and would have to suffer intensely before he could resolve it.

Monologues and dialogues: Poulenc's later music 1950-63

The death of Christian Bérard must have brought home to Poulenc how many of his friends, associates and the artists he admired had, beginning with Apollinaire, Radiguet and Raymonde Linossier, died tragic, painful or premature deaths. To the pre-war deaths, both violent, of Ferroud and García Lorca was now added a whole cortege of further sacrificial victims, martyrs to racial hatred and war: Max Jacob and Robert Desnos above all, the latter dying in Theresiendstadt concentration camp in 1945 and whose heart-rending 'Le Disparu' and 'Le Dernier Poème' Poulenc would set to music in 1947 and 1956 respectively, as well as such less well-known figures as the sculptor Fernand Ochsé and his wife Louise (both gassed at Auschwitz in 1944, having been put on the last train to leave Drancy before the Liberation of Paris) and the music publisher Raymond Deiss, publisher of many works by Les Six, who was executed – by decapitation – for Resistance activities in 1943. These deaths obviously made Poulenc think of earlier tragedies, like that of his friend, the painter and art critic Emmanuel Faÿ, who had committed suicide as long ago as 1923; his death was still felt acutely enough for Poulenc to dedicate one of *Calligrammes* (1948) to his memory. Nor did the end of hostilities bring any surcease. Bérard's death was preceded by that, at the age of 39, of the art dealer Pierre Colle to whose memory Poulenc would dedicate one of his settings of Jacob's *Parisiana* in 1954, and was followed, in 1952, by that of Paul Eluard, aged 57. Also in 1952, Poulenc's favourite conductor, Roger Désormière ('Déso', 1898-1963), had a stroke at the wheel of his car while driving in Italy. Left speechless, paralysed but still mentally alert, he would endure a decade-long calvary which would end only after Poulenc's own death; Poulenc, who visited him regularly, would find in his friend's terrible ordeal another example of expiatory suffering. The

violinist Ginette Neveu, who had given the premiere of Poulenc's Violin
Sonata in 1943, was killed in an aircrash over the Azores in October 1949,
while a still greater violinist friend, Jacques Thibaud, a former lover of
Germaine Tailleferre, also died in an aircrash in Indo-China in 1953. The
following year, Poulenc's last link with the world of Raymonde Linossier,
Adrienne Monnier, committed suicide, the victim of a disease of the inner ear
causing bouts of vertigo and unremitting tinnitus, and, the year after that, Les
Six became Les Cinq when, after a long illness, Arthur Honegger died.
Finally, in September 1957, the curse of the automobile struck again when
the great English horn player, Dennis Brain, whom Poulenc knew through
Britten and Pears, was killed in a car crash, inspiring Poulenc to produce one
of his most tragic and austere works, the Elegy for Horn and Piano (1957), in
his memory. If Poulenc's work is haunted by the omnipresence of violent,
tragic or premature death, the reason is in large part to be found in the
holocaust of his personal friends.

Les Mamelles de Tirésias was one of Poulenc's favourite amongst his own
compositions and marks the apotheosis of the *voyou* element within him. But,
despite the success of *Quatre petites prières de Saint Francis d'Assise* and the
Stabat Mater, his monkish other half was far less satisfied, and Poulenc in due
course contacted Guido Valcarenghi, director of the Milan-based music
publishers Ricordi, who proposed a ballet on the subject of the life of Saint
Margaret of Cortona (1247-97). Poulenc found little to inspire him in this
thirteenth-century tale of youthful sin, repentance and self-mortification, and
told Valcarenghi as much when he was in Milan in March 1953. To
Poulenc's hesitant proposal of an opera on a 'mystical' theme, Valcarenghi
immediately made the inspired suggestion of Bernanos's *Dialogues des
Carmélites* which Poulenc had in fact read and seen twice, without
considering it suitable material for an opera. Moving on to Rome, Poulenc
'happened' on a copy of the text in a bookshop window, bought it and re-
read it in one sitting on the *terrazza* of the Tre Scalini café on the Piazza
Navone. There, helped along by a coffee, an ice cream, an orange juice and a
bottle of Fuggi water, he took a long and complex passage from the text at
random and, to his amazement, immediately found the melodic line
appropriate to it; convinced that the piece was 'made for him', he telephoned

his acceptance back to Valcarenghi. In June 1953 he set out on his, by now, institutionalised pilgrimage of dedication to Rocamadour and, in the train from Paris to Brive, red biro in hand, made the necessary cuts and emendations to Bernanos's text. From the outset, Poulenc appears to have considered the composition of his 'mystical' opera as itself an act of mystical devotion. Having prayed to Saint Francis at Assisi just before going on to Milan, Poulenc undoubtedly regarded Valcarenghi's proposal of the *Dialogues* as providential, telling Bernac in September 1953, shortly after he began the actual writing of his work at Noizay, that, 'I have prayed so many hours for a libretto that the Holy Mother sent me this one to sing her praises with', and attributing his rapid early progress to her continuing intervention: 'Sublime weather, flowers ditto. [...] All in all, divine summer. Rocamadour has a lot to do with this, I *know*.' (C p. 761, B p. 208.) When, the following year, the writing became much more painful for reasons to be discussed, Poulenc consciously interpreted his personal and artistic difficulties in the light of the opera's themes of redemptive suffering, the reversibility of merits and the communion of saints. If *Dialogues des Carmélites* is such a great work, and one that should finally put paid to any idea of its composer as a self-evading purveyor of facetious *bonbons*, it is not least because, for much of its composition, Poulenc truly believed, as Bernanos had as he wrote the original text, that he was actually *living* the sacrificial ordeal that he was putting into music.

Dialogues des Carmélites has a complex prehistory, which it is necessary briefly to review in order to appreciate why Poulenc came to see it as 'tailor made' for his interests and needs. In 1931, the German novelist Gertrud von Le Fort (1876-1971) – a convert to Catholicism – published a novelle entitled *Die Letzte am Schafott (The Last to the Scaffold)* based on the 'true story' of 16 Carmelite sisters from Compiègne to the north-east of Paris who, on 17 July 1794, were condemned to death by Fouquier-Tinville's Revolutionary Tribunal for a variety of 'counter-revolutionary' offences and, later the same day, were guillotined on the Place du Trône Renversé (the present Place de la Nation); they are buried in the nearby Cimetière de Picpus and were beatified by Pope Pius X in May 1906. Deeply disturbed by the rise of Nazism in her country and by the failure of people like herself (and of

Catholics generally) to do anything to counter it, Le Fort came across an account of the sisters' martyrdom in Munich University library – probably that written by a surviving *consoeur*, Sister Marie de l'Incarnation, who figures prominently in both the novelle and Bernanos's play – and decided to use it as the historical framework in which to explore the dilemmas of a character closely modelled on herself to whom she gives the hardly fortuitous name of Blanche de la Force. The novelle is written in the form of a letter by a French nobleman 'Herr von Villeroi' to an *émigrée* and describes the life of the aristocratic Blanche from her tragic and violent birth in 1774 – swept up by a panicking crowd on the eve of the marriage of the future Louis XVI and Marie-Antoinette, her mother goes into premature labour and dies after giving birth – to her violent and tragic death 20 years later. As a result of the traumatic circumstances of her birth, Blanche is stricken with a pathological fear of virtually everything and, shortly before the outbreak of the Revolution, flees from herself as much as from 'the world' into the Carmel at Compiègne. There she starts to come to terms with her obsessions and phobias, but any prospect of security ends when the revolutionary government in Paris orders the dissolution of all religious orders and the closing of their houses, and the local 'patriots' accordingly begin to move in on the Carmel. At Mother Marie's instigation, the sisters take a vow of martyrdom rather than surrender to the revolutionaries' demands, whereupon Blanche, terror-struck once again, takes flight and returns to her father's mansion in Paris. There, however, still greater horrors await her. Not only does she witness her father's death at the hands of the mob but is forced to drink human blood from a chalice, and is finally taken by her captors to witness the execution of her fellow sisters, which Le Fort transfers to the Place de la Révolution (the present Place de la Concorde). One by one the sisters approach the guillotine singing the 'Veni Creator' until only one voice sustains the hymn. When this last voice is silenced, another rises from the crowd; it is Blanche, transcending her fear not through her own efforts but through divine grace and voluntarily identifying herself with her sisters, and she continues to sing until she is done to death by the mob. Entrusting herself entirely to God, she discovers that when she is weak, she is strong; the last to the scaffold, she is first in God's love.

Die Letzte am Schafott was translated into French in 1937, and *La Dernière à l'échafaud* was one of the few books that accompanied Bernanos when he took refuge in Brazil at the beginning of the Second World War. In 1947 he was approached by a Dominican friend, Father Brückberger, with a view to writing the dialogue for a film based on the novelle, of which he, Brückberger, had devised an outline scenario. Bernanos was by then living in Tunisia and did not have access to the original, so that the script which resulted differed in significant respects from Le Fort's novelle, not only in respect of form, characterisation and plot, but also in the theology that underpins it. Himself seriously ill – he would indeed take to his bed on the day he completed his text, in March 1948, dying just over three months later – Bernanos, working from Brückberger's scenario and memory alone, virtually rewrote the novelle in the light of his own personal and religious preoccupations. Any element of political allegory is dropped, making the surviving text distinctly reactionary in its ideological implications, and the development of certain scenes and characters foregrounds the themes of vicarious suffering and the communion of saints that are, at most, peripheral to Le Fort's psychological and political concerns. Above all, the whole text becomes haunted by death in a way that goes far beyond the already doom-laden original. Where Le Fort had merely noted the death of the first prioress of the Carmel Madame de Croissy, Bernanos makes it the pivotal scene of the first half of his script, bringing out the dying woman's inconsolable anguish with a poignancy that Poulenc's music would match and carry to still greater heights, and even giving her the same age as himself (59). He introduces the key secondary character, Sister Constance, who, plainly based on Saint Thérèse de Lisieux for whom he had a particular devotion, embodies that spirit of childlikeness which, for him, transcends every other Christian virtue, and gives closer attention to the debates between Mother Marie and both of the prioresses over the rights and wrongs of deliberate martyrdom; the blood-drinking scene is happily excised. The manuscript remained unpublished for several years after Bernanos's death, and was assembled for publication in 1951 by his friend and literary executor, the Swiss-born critic Albert Béguin (1901-57), yet another convert to Catholicism, who, *inter alia*, gave the work its telling present title. It was immediately evident, however, that Bernanos's dense, discursive text, though highly dramatic, was totally unsuited to the cinema, and it was first performed as a play – in German, under the title *Die Begnadete Angst* (*Blessed or Merciful Anguish*) – at Zürich in 1951, pending its premiere in Paris at the Théâtre Hébertot in May the following year. In 1960, the cinéast, Philippe Agostini, directed a film based on Brückberger's scenario and largely written by him (645 lines to 265 taken from Bernanos) which displeased Bernanos's admirers and sank into rapid oblivion. *Dialogues des Carmélites* is still occasionally performed as a play, but it is essentially in Poulenc's operatic recreation that the work survives.

In reworking Le Fort's novelle, Bernanos did much more than merely expand certain characters and scenes; he radically altered the work's underlying meaning, and, after seeing the German production of the play, Le Fort was moved to protest gently, but insistently, against his distortion – as she saw it – of her intentions. In an essay entitled 'Zu Georges Bernanos' "Die Begnadete Angst"', she stresses that, *for her*, Blanche's eventual triumph over fear results from the 'pure, almost incomprehensible grace [or mercy] of God' (*'die reine, fast unbegreifliche Gnade Gottes'*) whereas, for Bernanos, it is also God-given, not, to be sure, because *she* has deserved it, but because the prioress has merited it *for her* through the 'substitutive sacrifice' (*'das stellvertretende Opfer'*) of her agonising death;[80] put more simply, Blanche dies 'easily' and at peace with herself because the prioress endured such spiritual and physical anguish, the accrued 'merits' of which subsequently 'revert' to her *protégée*. Here, clearly stated, is the disturbing but, to many, inspiring Catholic doctrine of 'vicarious suffering', or 'mystical substitution', whereby the saint, following the ineffable example of Christ, *substitutes* himself – or herself – for sinners who would otherwise be damned and, by suffering for them in their place, redeems them 'vicariously' thanks to the mysterious 'reversibility' of merits and to the solidarity of the saints working in communion with each other for the salvation of sinful humanity. 'Mystical substitution' was the cornerstone of the theology of Bloy, Maritain, Huysmans and practically every other militant Catholic of the 'reactionary revolution', and Bernanos gives it especial authority by placing its most memorable formulation in the mouth of his Thérèse-figure, Sister Constance: 'We die not for ourselves alone but for one another, or sometimes even instead of each other, who knows.' (*'On ne meurt pas chacun pour soi, mais les uns pour les autres, ou même les uns à la place des autres, qui sait.')*[81] No matter that Thérèse herself rarely, if ever, fully endorsed the theory and practice of vicarious suffering, adopting a position on grace much closer to that of Le Fort. As reworked by Bernanos, the life and, above all, the death of Blanche de la Force becomes a manifesto for the doctrine of mystical substitution and was regarded as such by Poulenc himself. If *Dialogues des Carmélites* is virtually the doctrine's last appearance in literature, it is also, and especially when set to music by Poulenc, its most moving, as well as its most coherent, expression.

Devout to the point of superstitious, Poulenc began writing the music for *Dialogues des Carmélites* on the Feast of the Assumption (15 August) 1953. At first the music came to him with extraordinary ease – 'It just flows and flows,' (*'Cela vient, cela vient,'*) he told Bernac on 1 September, 'and it is like nobody but myself; it is madly vocal (*c'est follement vocal*)' (C p. 760) – and he made progress at the rate of one scene per week, thanks, he told another correspondent, to his 'familiarity with vocal music on the one hand, and with the mystical ambiance on the other' (C p. 766). But all Poulenc's experience would not have produced music of such passion and intensity had he not identified so closely with his characters, their situation and, above all, with the underlying themes and tone of Bernanos's text: 'If I am to succeed with this work,' he told Bernac on 22 August, 'it will only be through the music identifying absolutely with the Bernanos *spirit*.' 'I am crazy about my subject,' he wrote to another friend on 31 August, 'to the point of believing that I have actually known these women' (C p. 759); 'since 15 August, it has been Carmel at Noizay' (C p. 766). With male roles largely peripheral and functional, the 'feminine' in Poulenc was able to express itself more freely and fully than ever before, and in Blanche and the first prioress, Mme de Croissy, he found the ideal female personae through which he could voice his own inveterate fears and anxieties; their first encounter at the Carmel yields, as he rightly says, music 'astounding in its calmness, severity, peacefulness and violence' (C p. 759). Blanche is, in effect, Poulenc's female alter ego. He was, in his own words, *'un éternel inquiet'* (C p. 976), and in Blanche he found an embodiment of all his own depressive tendencies and phobias, his recurring bouts of morbid self-criticism verging at times on utter self-contempt, the whole thing made worse, rather than alleviated, by his equally profound spiritual aspirations. In the case of the prioress, pathological anxiety becomes outright metaphysical anguish, and there is no scene in the opera, not even the conclusion, that produces music of greater intensity than that of her utterly disconsolate, but all too public, death-agonies in which, pushed to the extremity, she accuses God of abandoning her at the hour when, after a lifetime of prayer and obedience, she has greatest need of Him: 'Let Him first concern Himself with me!' *('Que suis-je à cette heure, moi misérable, pour m'inquiéter de lui! Qu'il s'inquiète donc d'abord de moi!')* It is, as Poulenc says, 'the crux of the whole play' (C p. 777), the first and most important of its several re-enactments of Gethsamene and Golgotha, and on it turns the whole drama of Blanche's eventual salvation. Despite growing compositional difficulties ; 'Sanctity is difficult enough,' he told Yvonne Gouverné, 'but sacred music of the Carmelites kind is terrifying' (C p. 769) – Poulenc completed the scene at Lausanne in the week before Christmas 1953, and, 'exhausted but very relieved,' decided to 'take a little breather' before pressing on, optimistic, and with reason, that he would be able to finish the whole work, orchestration included, in the course of the following year (C p. 777). As it turned out, 1954 would be Poulenc's year of personal calvary, and his life and the opera on which he was working would start to interact with each other in uncanny ways, so that, before long, the composer came to believe that he was actually living through the drama of redemptive suffering and the transfer of grace that he rightly identified as the *Dialogues*' psychological and spiritual core (see ECR p. 213).

At first, the process of composition continued to go well, despite miserable weather (at Cannes of all places) and growing personal unhappiness, both of which Poulenc, beneath his jocular tone, believed to have been sent by 'his ladies' (*'mes dames'*) as a creative incentive: 'I think it is those Carmelite nuns who have exacted this austerity from on high.' (C p. 782.) By mid-February he told his friend and biographer, Henri Hell, that he was 'horribly sad', though once again he accepted the unhappiness as a necessary stimulus to creation: 'No doubt this anguished climate was necessary for my nuns. [...] I would never have believed that I could write a work in this style. I thank God for it, despite the suffering involved. And yet with all that suffering, I will still be known as "the charming Poulenc".' (C p. 785, B p. 216.) The first act of the *Dialogues* was completed in March 1954 while Poulenc was on concert tour with Bernac in Egypt, whereafter the published correspondence, a long letter to Bernac in July (?) 1954, becomes brief and fragmentary, suggesting that something like a complete breakdown, or at least a major physical, emotional and spiritual crisis, had occurred, without, however, its incapacitating Poulenc the artist. The crisis seems to have originated in the complexity, even the duplicity, of Poulenc's personal life whence it rapidly enveloped both his physical and spiritual being. Some time in the late 1940s, Poulenc had formed an emotional and physical attachment with a man some ten years younger than himself, Lucien Roubert (1908(?)-1955), whom he had met in the latter's home town of Toulon. The relationship was pursued whenever Poulenc came to the Midi, notwithstanding his continuing involvement – by now probably platonic – with his driver Raymond Destouches while at home in the Touraine; the letter to Bernac also hints at an abiding affection for the painter and art dealer, Richard Chanlaire, in Paris. In April 1954, Raymond seems to have moved, or to have threatened to move, out of Le Grand Coteau back into the village of Noizay, and Lucien too seems to have distanced himself from Poulenc at much the same time; perhaps each had somehow heard of the other and acted accordingly. The possibility of losing his two closest companions more or less simultaneously threw Poulenc, in his own words, into a 'blind panic that was not helped at all by worries about my liver, about my faith' – evidently, his *foie* and his *foi* were equally delicate – and, not least, about an increasingly vexatious dispute with an American author over rights to any stage production based on *Die Letzte am Schafott* 'which means that I may be writing a work that can never be performed'.[82] Torn between his 'consuming love for Lucien' and his 'limitless affection for Raymond', knowing that he had betrayed both and risked preserving the affections of neither, Poulenc agreed with Bernac that he had indeed 'poisoned myself little by little. Too much introspection – emotional as well as intellectual – has been gnawing away at me for months. But can one prevent a lame man from limping?' 'Six weeks of near mad anxiety' had produced the usual psychosomatic effects – inflamed tonsils, 'and what this has done to the level of my uric acid is unimaginable' – and a recent pilgrimage to Lourdes ('atrocious and sublime') had done nothing to alleviate the symptoms; perhaps forthcoming visits to Rocamadour and Ligugé, the

Benedictine abbey near Poitiers much favoured by Huysmans, Claudel and Rouault as a place of retreat, would renew him in body and mind. His one consolation was that all this misery and stress had not destroyed his creativity. Indeed, they seemed even to have heightened it, for at one 'extraordinary moment of emotion and turmoil [...] the final moments of the Carmelites came to me, Blanche's arrival and her march to the scaffold. Looking at this music coldly, I honestly believe that it is overwhelming in its simplicity, in its resignation, and ... in its peace.' (C pp. 796-8, B pp. 219-20.) Similarly, in a letter of March 1957, Poulenc disclosed to another friend that 'the angelic Ave Maria' which follows the election of the new prioress, Mme Lidoine, 'was composed on one day in January 1954 when I was miserable because Lucien had stood me up (*m'avait posé un lapin*)' (C p. 863). The key theme of the *Dialogues* is the inscrutable link between suffering and grace; in writing his opera, Poulenc discovered how his own sufferings – less acute, to be sure, than those of his 'ladies', but all the more humiliating for that – might, without his conscious volition, be transformed into his own version of the Carmelites' song on the scaffold.

All this was lost on the loyal, but exasperated, Bernac, who, in a letter of November 1954, took Poulenc roundly to task and told him, in effect, to snap out of it. Just as his misery was all of his own making, so too the solution lay in his hands:

> Unfortunately, through your lack of moral virility, you have worn down the affection of this loyal but not very interesting boy [Roubert]. I am sorry for you if you really love him as much as you think you do, something of which I am not entirely convinced. You loved the character you wanted him to play at your side. If you had really loved him you would have loved him for himself and not for you. But that was not the case. As proof I merely observe that before this breakup you would not have hesitated to form other attachments, yet you were jealous of any he might have made. [...] Face the reality plainly and squarely and put up with it. You are neither the first nor the last to suffer a broken heart. It is too convenient, don't you see, to put everything down to illness. Your inclination to let yourself go does not date from today. What is more, there is

GEORGES BERNANOS

Dialogues des Carmélites

*E sienplaire de mon
decompinje .
Fr. Poulenc*

Les Cahiers du Rhône
AUX ÉDITIONS DU SEUIL

THE TITLE PAGE OF POULENC'S COPY OF GEORGES BERNANOS'
DIALOGUES DES CARMÉLITES

human dignity to be preserved. I suffer so much to see you losing it completely in the eyes of everyone, not only your friends. Francis Poulenc, even on the human plane, is surely greater than this. Have no doubt that this feebleness will eventually make itself felt in your art. Life is not a matter of easy solutions.

C p. 810, B p. 225

But, far from 'snapping out of it', Poulenc cut short a scheduled concert tour in Germany and admitted himself into a private clinic at L'Hay-les-Roses in the southern *banlieue* of Paris and there, with the help of drugs, proceeded to sleep 18 or 19 hours a day to make up for months of insomnia: 'Not much fun but there was no choice.' (C p. 811.) By December, he was starting to emerge from his 'black hole', but the 'joyous Poulenc of old' seemed lost for ever (C p. 814). Then, after a trip to England in January 1955 where he performed his Concerto for Two Pianos with Britten at the Royal Festival Hall, things took an unexpected turn for the worst, and Poulenc's whole life became, for several months, a re-enactment *en plus petit* of the metaphysical drama of 'his ladies'.

In February 1955, Poulenc learned that Roubert was suffering from tuberculosis. His condition was not yet critical, a reconciliation occurred, and Poulenc supervised his hospitalisation in Toulon, visiting him whenever his crowded schedule permitted. By July, Roubert seemed to have made a recovery, and it was now Poulenc who became ill once again. 'I hope I have saved him' (*'J'espère l'avoir sauvé'*), he wrote a friend from Evian where he had gone for a cure, adding that 'now suddenly the tables have turned, but all this is too complicated to tell you here' (C p. 821, B p. 230 (slightly modified)) – too complicated, perhaps, because Poulenc seems to be describing the doctrine of mystical substitution at work: Lucien gets ill, Francis suffers with him, Lucien gets better, Francis becomes ill, as the 'turning tables' of vicarious suffering move endlessly this way and that. But, at Evian, Poulenc himself made a notable recovery and was able to resume composing ('my menopause is over', as he significantly put it (C p. 825)) – which, if the remorseless logic of the doctrine of substitution is true (I suffer, you prosper; I prosper, you suffer), implies that Lucien's condition would once more deteriorate. This indeed is what happened, and, in August, Poulenc had the now desperately sick Roubert transferred to a clinic in Cannes where, staying as usual at the Hotel Majestic, he planned to work on the remaining scenes of the *Dialogues*, before moving back to Noizay to write the climactic song at the scaffold. A letter of the time to Bernac indicates Poulenc's complete acceptance of the theology underpinning his opera:

> I have entrusted [Lucien] to my 16 blessed Carmelites: may they protect his final hours since he has been so closely involved with their story. In fact I began the work at his side, in happiness, in Lyons in August 1953. After all the torment, which I need not describe to you, I have just finished the work, at his side, during the last days of his earthly life. As I wrote to you once before, I am haunted by Bernanos's phrase: 'We do not die for ourselves alone ... but for, or instead of, each other.' If Raymond [Destouches] remains the secret of *Les Mamelles* and *figure humaine*, Lucien is certainly that of the *Stabat* and *Les Carmélites*.

Of course, Poulenc was simplifying and exaggerating for effect: the *Dialogues* were not finished, nor had they been begun at Lyons with Roubert but in solitude at Noizay. But the basic point stands: Francis and Lucien have lived through, together, the opera's theme of redemptive substitution and suffering, now Lucien is dying, and 'this great great drama of my life' – Poulenc means his love for Lucien, but the *Dialogues* are also implied – 'is ending in the most melancholy (dare I say it) happiness' (C pp. 825-6, B p. 232). Rarely can there have been so close a convergence between the explicit message of a work and the experience its creator lived through as he wrote it.

When, as he must often have during this time, Poulenc considered the lives and deaths of the artists he had known and admired, from *le poète assassiné* (Apollinaire) to *le poète disparu* (Desnos) and beyond, he cannot have failed to remark how suffering, death and creativity were as intimately linked for the poet, the painter, and the composer, as suffering, death and redemption were for the sisters of the Compiègne Carmel. Now he had a dying lover on his mind (not to say on his conscience) as he worked on the climactic scenes of his opera at Noizay. The story of its completion is well known and, even allowing for some myth-making on Poulenc's part, it rings essentially true. After Poulenc left Cannes, Roubert had been transferred back to hospital in Toulon, and it was there that he finally died on 15 October 1955, the very day – if we believe Poulenc's several accounts – that the vocal score of the *Dialogues* was finished four or five hundred kilometres to the north:

> Lucien [was] delivered from his martyrdom ten days ago, the final copy of *Les Carmélites* [being] completed (take note) at the very moment the poor boy breathed his last. I got up from the table and said to my faithful Anna [the housekeeper at Noizay]: 'I have finished: Monsieur Lucien will die now.' Who will ever know all that lies at the secret heart of certain works? [...] I hope that when my time comes, I shall know how to die ... as Blanche did.
>
> C p. 831, B p. 236

I have finished, it is finished: Lucien is the Christ-figure who gives up the ghost at the very instant that the work his suffering made possible is completed. A year later, close to the anniversary of Lucien's death, Poulenc makes the Christological analogy even plainer:

> Naturally, my thoughts often revolve around Lucien, and, although I have made total peace with his memory, the notion that he may have died in my place, and from what I believed I was suffering from, troubles me deeply.
>
> C p. 847, B p. 242

Human lives and human deaths are all interconnected. There is a communion of sinners as well as a communion of saints, and merits and demerits, health and sickness, life and death, circulate endlessly through the body of the Church, to the ultimate greater good of the whole. The Catholic world is a reversible world, in which no-one is alone and no-one 'owns' his or her merit or salvation. Only God gives, everything else is exchanged and, as the

POULENC WORKING AT HIS PIANO AT NOIZAY AROUND 1950

priest-confessor of the Carmel tells Blanche (in a passage not set by Poulenc), 'one is always unworthy of what one receives [...], for one never receives but from God'; all are members of each other, but only because Christ was dismembered on the Cross and has been re-membered ever since in the sacraments. Together, Gethsamene and Golgotha found the Catholic community, and it is this originary sacrifice that the Carmelite sisters are called upon to re-enact as their part in the mystery of 'universal redemption'.

Until the final scenes of the *Dialogues*, Poulenc had followed the basic structure of Bernanos's text, deleting a great deal to streamline the action, inserting two exquisite hymns, the 'Ave Maria' and the 'Ave Verum Corpus', at significant points of transition, and transferring the whole scene of the breaking of the Petit Roi de Gloire – the statue of the Child Jesus with its obvious echoes of Thérèse that Blanche, terrified by the singing of the 'Carmagnole' outside, drops when it is brought to her cell on Christmas Eve – to a later stage in the drama, where the incident's sacrificial significance stands out with far greater force. But as Bernanos, himself gravely ill, hastened to finish his text, he left its conclusion in a schematic and somewhat confused state, thus allowing Poulenc to go beyond setting another's words to music (and enhancing them in the process) to engage in further creative transpositions of his own. In the scene in the Conciergerie in which the second prioress addresses her charges, he maximises the moment's Christological resonance by giving to the prioress words – and a sublime melody to match them – that, in the Bernanos version, were uttered earlier on by Sisters Marthe and Claire: 'Standing on the Mount of Olives, Christ Himself was no longer master. He knew the fear of death.' This, in its turn, gives much greater salience to Sister Constance's question that follows immediately after – 'and what of Sister Blanche?' – and enables Poulenc to foreground the pivotal role, clearly intended by Bernanos, of the most childlike of the sisters in Blanche's salvation. Constance has already taken Blanche's fears on herself when, in the memorable scene in which the sisters, under the instigation of Mother Marie de l'Incarnation, are required to vote for or against martyrdom, she voted against – and made public she had done so – in order to protect 'Blanche de la Faiblesse' from accusations of cowardice. Now she expresses her certainty that Blanche will return from hiding to share in their martyrdom and, when asked why she is so sure, answers 'because ... because ...' – the sisters break into giggles that are rapidly silenced by the entrance of the gaoler – 'because of a dream that I've had'; again the music is of such heart-rending innocence and confidence that the Thérèse-like beauty of Constance – 'of course I am in love with Sister Constance', Poulenc had told Bernac soon after beginning the work (C p. 761) – is highlighted in a way that the original text never really achieves. To emphasise the horror of what is about to occur, Poulenc then departs entirely from Bernanos's scenario and has the gaoler bark out the names of the condemned sisters one after the other – 15 names in all, for Blanche's is missing – and then, in a monstrous prostitution of language by ideology and bureaucracy, enumerates the crimes of which they have been found guilty: formenting 'counter-revolutionary conventicles' ('conciliabules'), engaging in 'fanatical correspondence' and hoarding 'liberticidal writings', all against a cacophany of piano, drums, skirling strings and flatulent brass that renders the gaoler's staccato roll-call still more machine-like and sinister. Absent when her 'daughters' voted in favour of martyrdom, the prioress urges them to accept death in humility, as from the hands of God, whereupon the scene shifts to a street close to the former site of the Bastille where the father-confessor informs Mother Marie of the sisters' condemnation. Having actively *willed* martyrdom, and organised the vote in its favour, the sub-prioress considers herself 'dishonoured' at not sharing – and not being *seen* to share – the fate of her sisters, and is roundly upbraided by the father-confessor for her pride and continuing bondage to the opinion of 'the world'; her martyrdom will be *not* to be martyred but to survive, and to pass on to posterity the story of the Carmelites of Compiègne, so making possible their eventual beatification, not to mention the celebration of their humility by Le Fort, Bernanos – and Poulenc. Even the proud and ambitious cooperate unknowingly with God in the creation of the communion of saints.

Having clarified the opera's psychology, history and theology, Poulenc can now move on to its climactic song at the scaffold. Here the composer has by definition the advantage over the novelist-dramatist, for Bernanos's last scene contains no dialogue, only a bare description of what happens on the Place de la Révolution. The crowd packs round the base of the scaffold, amongst them the father-confessor wearing a red, revolutionary bonnet to conceal his identity; as the sisters descend from the tumbrel, he murmurs absolution, makes a furtive sign of the cross and slips away into the crowd. Together singing the 'Salve Regina' in 'firm, clear voices', followed by the 'Veni Creator', the condemned women mount the scaffold and file one by one towards the guillotine. When only one sister remains – Bernanos does not specify her identity – another voice rises from the crowd, 'clear and more resolute than the others, with, however, something childlike about it (*avec pourtant quelque chose d'enfantin*)', and, to the amazement of the crowd, 'little Blanche de la Force' advances to the scaffold, her face seemingly 'devoid of all fear'. A group of women surrounds her and pushes her towards the scaffold, but she dies, singing the 'Veni Creator' until the very last instant, before she can reach it, apparently pummelled and kicked to death by the women; as in the Le Fort original, Bernanos's Blanche is a victim *not* of the guillotine but of (female) mob violence. To this scenario Poulenc makes a number of significant alterations and additions. He has Sister Constance jump 'almost joyfully' from the tumbrel, and specifies that it is she who is the last of the 15 women to go to the guillotine. As she does so, singing the 'Salve Regina' at the top of her voice, she sees Sister Blanche emerge, as she had prophesied, from the mass of the crowd, her face is 'flooded with happiness' and she 'smiles sweetly' at her sister in Christ until the falling blade of the guillotine brutally truncates her song; it is the beatific smile of the Virgin, eclipsing and staunching all tears, as the two child-sisters of Jesus are reunited at the moment of death. But Poulenc's principal innovation is to have Blanche herself mount the scaffold and die by the guillotine rather than at the hands of the mob. His reasons for doing so were not only, or even primarily, dramatic. By having Blanche decapitated by the revolutionary state, Poulenc underlines the properly sacrificial character of her death; she is the victim of deranged ideology and officialised paranoia rather than simply of the hysteria of the mob. But, as a number of critics have remarked,[83] Blanche's decapitation replicates the decapitation of the 'martyred' Ferroud whose death was instrumental in leading Poulenc back to the Church or, as the theology of mystical substitution would put it, his death was the 'ransom' that purchased or redeemed the life of his friend. The repeated, sickening thud of the guillotine blade in the opera's last scene re-enacts the sacrificial death of a feminised fellow musician whose voice was cut off with the violence and finality of those of Sisters Constance and Blanche: *O pia, o dulcis Virgo Ma …* Also feminised, Poulenc-*voyou* and Poulenc-*moine* likewise meet and merge in the reunion of Constance and Blanche on the scaffold, and, simultaneously, Poulenc identifies both with the martyred musician to whose death he owes his conversion and with the martyred ex-lover whose illness and death presided over, and made possible, the elaboration of his work. But in the end it is Blanche-Ferroud-Roubert who dies, not Poulenc himself; like Mother Marie, he lives on, the artist, to testify – martyr means witness in Greek – and so bring to completion the mystery of redemption that the opera enacts. Dedicated to the memory of his mother 'who revealed music to me', to Debussy 'who gave me the inclination (*le goût*) to write it' and to Monteverdi, Verdi and Mussorgsky 'who served here as my masters' (ECR pp. 211-12)[84], *Dialogues des Carmélites* brings together the masculine and the feminine, the *moine* and the *voyou*, in a supreme musical celebration, both tragic and joyful, of the *mysterium magnum* of grace. Not for nothing does the opera have as its epigraph 'this fiery statement (*cette phrase brûlante*) of Saint Theresa [of Avila]: "May God deliver me from gloomy saints."'[85] The most tragic and least gloomy of works, *Dialogues des Carmélites* finally attains that holy simplicity which the dying prioress, in a passage not set by Poulenc, describes as 'a gift of childhood which, most frequently, does not survive childhood .... Once out of childhood, one must suffer at great length in order to return to it, just as, at the end of the night, one discovers a new dawn. Have I become a child again? (*Suis-je redevenue enfant?*)' Poulenc had never lost that spirit of childhood but, like Blanche, he had often been childish rather than childlike. Now, having suffered, he was able to synthesise the *moine* and the *voyou* and, through the voice of his 'ladies', create one of the most truly Catholic – and catholic – works of the twentieth century.

'Whoever enters Gethsemane never emerges again' (the first prioress in *Dialogues des Carmélites*). If Poulenc hoped that he had finished once and for all with his personal and metaphysical anguish in completing *Dialogues des Carmélites*, his relief was short-lived for, in February 1958, just over a year after the opera's first performance at La Scala (January 1957), he ascended his individual Mount of Olives again with a work that has been rightly described as a secular 'appendix' to the *Dialogues*, but one which proves to be 'hardly less purgatorial' than its sacred predecessor.[86] This is *La Voix humaine*, an orchestral setting of almost the whole of Cocteau's one-act *tour de force* of the same title featuring just the woman's side of a desperate telephone conversation between her and a lover who has betrayed her. First performed at the Comédie-Française in February 1930, the play was widely interpreted at the time as an unanswered monologue addressed by Cocteau *outre-tombe* to the spirit of Radiguet or, more wickedly, as a scarcely disguised plea and reproach to the author's current flighty companion Jean Desbordes (see the third chapter); 'it's obscene,' Eluard is said to have bellowed at the premiere, 'enough, enough, it's Desbordes that you're phoning!' For his part, Poulenc did not conceal his identification with the speaker. 'Blanche was me, and she is me also,' he wrote to one correspondent, and to another repeated Flaubert's all too familiar '*Madame Bovary, c'est moi*'; the 'atrocious tragedy' is 'my own', and the work is a 'musical confession', though it would be an error to attach too precise an identity to the unseen and unheard lover on the other end of the line (C pp. 890–5). It might be one more prayer to the extraterrestrial spirit of Lucien Roubert or a plea to Poulenc's current companion, the rather more down-to-earth 'Louis the builder', whom he had met in March 1957[87] and who was with him when he began the 'mono-opera' in Saint-Raphaël and Cannes. But the drama is set in what Cocteau calls the 'room of a murder (*chambre de meurtre*)', and the woman's winding of the telephone cord around her neck like a noose, plus the frequent references to the 'cutting off' of the callers, might have suggested once more the presence-absence of the decapitated Ferroud; Cocteau's stage directions even have the woman kneeling 'with her head cut off *(la tête coupeé)*' behind the back of a chair.[88] But *La Voix humaine* is more than coded autobiography. It is Poulenc's heart of the heartless world, his 'My God, my God, why hast thou forsaken me?', addressed from the cross of personal suffering to whoever – human being, God, or Christ – might hear it, a cry closer to the anguished plaint of the dying first prioress than to the joyful swansong of Sisters Constance and Blanche.

Poulenc was obviously aware of the parallels between his sacred opera and its secular successor, telling Louis Aragon that he, 'needed the experience of the spiritual and metaphysical anguish of *Les Carmélites* to avoid betraying the

POULENC AND JEAN COCTEAU IN THE SUMMER OF 1962

terribly human anguish of Jean Cocteau's superb text' (C p. 907, B p. 258). As usual when he found a text that spoke to his deepest instincts and needs, Poulenc wrote *La Voix humaine* at great speed, between February and June 1958, in what he describes as a 'state of trance'. But, almost as much as the songs that he wrote with, and for, Bernac, *La Voix humaine* was an act of co-creation with Denise Duval who, having sung the part of Blanche at the premier of the *Dialogues*, now took the sole role in the 'beautiful, sad child' she and Poulenc had brought together into the world (see the fourth chapter). Frequent musical, as well as thematic, echoes of the *Dialogues* justify calling the woman's ordeal (which includes an earlier suicide attempt) as 'a sacrificial act comparable, in private rather than public terms, with the nuns' communal relinquishment'[89] with the proviso that her 'martyrdom', unlike that of sisters Constance and Blanche, lacks any kind of transcendental significance and appears devoid of redemptive potential either for herself or her devious lover. The receiver falling to the ground as, sobbing *'Coupe!* (Cut!) *coupe vite! coupe! Je t'aime, je t'aime, je t'aime, je t'aime'*, she clutches the telephone to her breast, is a poor substitute for the severed heads of the sisters falling into the executioner's basket. Eros is not Agape, even experienced *usque ad mortem*, and her sufferings remain untransfigured by grace, while those of the sisters earn them beatitude.

After completing *La Voix humaine*, Poulenc returned to a choral work for male voices that he had begun in 1957 but left unfinished. The *Laudes de Saint Antoine de Padoue* are dedicated to the most famous of Saint Francis's disciples for whom Poulenc claimed to have had an 'extraordinary devotion' since 'tenderest childhood' when a 'great ugly greenish statue' of the saint adorned his bedroom. While Catholics traditionally invoke Saint Anthony's help in finding lost objects, Poulenc told Rostand that he, 'merely asks him to help me find myself (*me faire me retrouver moi-même*), and I am counting greatly on him, at the hour of my death, to aid me in the great crossing (*le grand passage*).' (ECR pp. 158-9.) If this is so, the miracle-making saint seems not yet to have delivered, for the least that can be said of the spare, disjointed music of the *Laudes* is that it does not suggest a man in happy possession of himself. Having been briefly exorcised by the writing of the *Dialogues*, the melancholic in Poulenc seemed to have reasserted its grip, and his next major

FROM LEFT: PETER PEARS, POULENC AND BENJAMIN BRITTEN
AT CANNES IN THE MID-1950S

work, the *Gloria*, written between May and December 1959, seems to have been undertaken with the explicit object of breaking with the generally doom-laden character of his more recent music. He wrote to Simone Girard in June 1959:

> What is necessary now is to be on target with the *Gloria*. Enough pain, enough passion. One must concede that from the *Stabat* to *La Voix*, life has not been a laughing matter. I think I needed all those painful experiences [...] to prove myself, but I have had enough now. Peace! ... peace!

> C p. 917, B p. 262

More than any other piece the *Gloria* fuses, rather than oscillates between, the *moine* and the *voyou*, and it is hardly surprising that the work was Poulenc's own favourite, and has continued to be that of the public as well; the whole composition, and the second part, the ebullient *Laudamus te*, in particular, was written with 'those frescoes by Gozzoli where the angels stick out their tongues' in mind, along with 'some serious Benedictine monks I had once seen revelling in a game of football' (see B p. 403). In 1954, one of Poulenc's spiritual advisers, Father Carré, had likened him to the tumbler-hero of Massenet's opera *Le Jongleur de Notre Dame* (1902) who, having fled public derision into a monastery where he is accused of blasphemy by the monks, dances himself to death before a statue of the Virgin, whose arm miraculously stretches out to bless him as he dies (C p. 797). In the *Gloria*, the ageing and perennially sickly Poulenc, whom even his closest friend Bernac compared to Watteau's Gilles with his 'hanging arms', 'large nose and enormous ears', 'strange walk, feet turned outwards' and 'profusion of woollens, shawls and rugs',[90] became, for a moment, an inspired sacred *jongleur*; no other modern Catholic music so uninhibitedly '[dances] before the Lord with all [its] might' (II Samuel: 6, 14).

The enormous success of the *Gloria*, especially in the United States where it had its world premiere, in Poulenc's presence, in January 1961, contributed greatly to the outward calm of the composer's final years; at the very least, he told Bernac, it and the *Stabat Mater* might 'spare me a few days of purgatory, if I narrowly avoid going to hell' (C p. 990). Spending much of his time at Bagnols-en-Forêt in the Var where 'Louis the builder' – in fact a career sergeant by profession who, in Poulenc's words, '[smiled] out at life with all his being' (C p. 874) – had singlehandedly built them a house, Poulenc experienced greater personal happiness than ever before, though the music he wrote during this Indian summer hardly exudes the 'confidence and calm' with which Sisters Constance and Blanche confronted their fate. Each of the two vocal scores he completed in the last two years of his life is haunted by loneliness, failure and death, though in tone and musical form they could not be more unalike. *La Dame de Monte-Carlo*, written in April 1961 at Monte-Carlo itself, is a setting for soprano and orchestra of a text that Cocteau had written in the 1930s for the cabaret singer Marianne Oswald (1903-85); Poulenc probably turned to it in memory of his stay in Monte-Carlo with Cocteau in January 1924 (see the third chapter). Embracing, in the composer's words, 'melancholy, pride, lyricism, violence and sarcasm' and, at its end, 'miserable tenderness [and] anguish' (J p. 63), the piece tells of an elderly *évaporeé* who, after a final spree in the casinos, flings herself into the Mediterranean; once again, Poulenc has found the ideal female voice, sardonic, self-pitying and defiant, through which to express his own faintly absurd excess of melancholy. The second work is altogether more serious – so serious, in fact, that Poulenc made his final pilgrimage to Rocamadour, in the summer of 1960, before setting to work on it, 'not without fear', as he confided to Bernac at the time (C p. 947). Written for boy soprano, mixed male chorus and full orchestra, the *Sept répons des ténèbres* are Poulenc's most extended musical meditation on the experience of Gethsemane and Golgotha, and are regarded by some critics as a greater work even than the *Gloria*. 'I thought it would be like Zurbarán but it has turned out to be like Mantegna,' Poulenc told Milhaud in May 1961 (C p. 980). The two painters, he said, 'correspond very closely to my religious ideal – the one with his mystical realism; the other with his ascetic purity that still permits him at times, without a qualm, to dress his women saints as ladies of fashion.' (C p. 960.) Poulenc is undoubtedly thinking of Mantegna's great *Cristo in scruto* (1480?) in the Pinacotheca di Brera in Milan which the art-loving composer is almost certain to have visited when in that city in March 1953 (see p. 90, above): 'The soles of its feet turned towards the spectators and in a foreshortened perspective, the corpse imposes itself [...] with a brutality bordering on the obscene.'[91] But, in an earlier letter to Bernac (C p. 960), Poulenc had mentioned not only Mantegna and Zurbarán but Holbein, the reference almost certainly being to that painter's extraordinary *Dead Christ* (1522) in Bâle Museum that so devastated Dostoyevsky when he saw it in 1867: 'That picture!' exclaims his parodic Christ-figure Myshkin in *The Idiot* (1868-9). 'Why some people may loose their faith by looking at that picture!' Here, in a painting seven to nine times longer than it is high, the vertical, transcendent dimension is suppressed absolutely, as is the presence of the women who weep in one corner of the *Cristo in scruto*; the emaciated body of the son of God lies stretched out, unmourned and abandoned, like the corpse of a drowned man on a mortician's slab. The text of Poulenc's seventh *responsum*, selected by himself from the liturgical corpus, transcribes this God- and man-forsaken death into words – *'Ecce quomodo moritur justus et nemo percipit corde'* ('Behold how the just man dies and no-one sees it in his heart') – which the composer then sets to music of unrelieved bleakness. Any consoling female presence is banished from this 20-minute meditation on betrayal and desertion: no Mother stands at the foot of the Cross to watch over her Son as He dies in utter dereliction, abandoned not only by His disciples but by His Father in Heaven. For once, Poulenc chooses to express the anguish of the martyr not through the voice of a woman but through that of a boy; it is as though, as for Thérèse, the crucified Christ becomes a child once again, with neither Father nor mother to sustain Him, *'tanquam agnus coram tondente se abmutuit et non aperuit os suum',* ('He was led as a sheep to the slaughter; and like a lamb dumb before his shearer, so opened he not his mouth,' Acts 8: 32), as in Zurbarán's stunning painting of the trussed-up, trembling *Lamb of God* (c. 1636-40) that he may have known in reproduction. The utterly forsaken Christs of Mantegna, Holbein and Zurbarán, the Lamb cowering in silence beneath the blade: how not to think, one final time, of the martyred bodies of Ferroud, Jacob, Desnos and Roubert and so many other of his friends?

Poulenc died suddenly of a heart attack in his apartment on the Rue Médicis on 30 January 1963, a few months before the death of his friend Jean Cocteau (13 October 1963) and, extraordinarily, on the thirty-third anniversary of the

POULENC IN HIS STUDY AT NOIZAY IN THE 1950S

death of the 33-year-old Raymonde Linossier. Four days before his death, after giving a recital with Denise Duval at Maastricht in Holland, he had sent flowers to her hotel room with a card saying *'Ma Denise, je te dois ma dernière joie* (I owe you the last of my joys)' (C p. 1008): he could at least address Denise as *'tu'*. Poulenc's death probably saved him from a further bout of heartbreak, as 'Louis the builder' was preparing to sell the house at Bagnols and become the manager of a bar in Cannes. Believers in the doctrine of mystical substitution – if, by then, there were any left in France other than Maritain and himself – would probably claim that his end was eased by the merits 'earned' by Ferroud and Roubert. He was buried at his local parish church, the Eglise Saint-Sulpice, and, like many others present, François Mauriac was surprised, and at first disappointed, that no music by Poulenc himself, not even the *Litanies à la Vierge noire*, was played at the service. Then Mauriac realised the profound beauty of the silence of the composer's voice before the ancient liturgy of the Church. 'A true sinner, by which I mean a true Christian', this 'false *mauvais garçon*' had, at the last, relinquished his individual voice, like Constance and Blanche singing the 'Salve Regina' and the 'Veni Creator' on the scaffold, to the universal voice of the Church, just as Poulenc's own music, and the church in which his requiem mass was celebrated, 'innovates less than it continues, is replete with an exalted spirituality, and yet with a charm, a grace and a frivolity which is at bottom nothing other than modesty, *une pudeur*.'[92]

Conclusion

How central was Poulenc's homosexuality to the music he wrote? That it was central to his *life* can hardly be doubted. Setting aside his wholly platonic love-from-afar for Raymonde Linossier (and in the absence of any published information at all about his relationship with the mother of his child), all the passionate and enduring attachments he formed during his adult life had men as their object: Richard Chanlaire, Raymond Destouches, Lucien Roubert, and the surname-less Louis and Claude of his later years. There were, in addition, a number of fleeting romances – one with 'un jeune *clergyman*' in Boston in 1950 ('I don't care for priests (*la prêtrise*) for that kind of thing', (C p. 672)) – plus an indeterminable amount of cruising, but nothing, surely, to justify Benjamin Ivry's claim that he lived 'a voracious gay sex life';[93] even when in the supposed pederasts' paradise of inter-war Tunisia and Algeria in 1935, Poulenc found himself returning 'mournful and anxious to my adventureless bedrooms (*mes chambres sans histoires*)' (C p. 404). Many of Poulenc's closest friends in the musical, literary and theatrical world were gay (Cocteau, Jacob, Sauguet, Bérard), and he had a particularly large number of gay friends abroad: Britten and Pears in England, Bernstein, Samuel Barber, Virgil Thomson and 'les *kiddies*' (Arthur Gold and Robert Fizdale) in the United States, and he was regularly visited by the gay American composer Ned Rorem during the latter's eventful five years in Paris (1951-56).[94] On the other hand, his crucial musical influences were all heterosexual rather than gay:[95] Debussy, Satie and Stravinsky and emphatically not (to take the obvious example) Ravel and '*le ravélisme*' whose 'yoke' – Poulenc's word – he and his fellow members of Les Six were anxious to shake off in favour of the 'proteiform' influence of Stravinsky (A p. 120). Similarly, it was poems by Apollinaire and Eluard, not Jacob, Cocteau or Lorca, that inspired Poulenc's finest songs, and Bernanos, not Cocteau, who provided the text for the greatest of his three works for the stage.

As far as its non-musical themes are concerned, Poulenc's work lacks the easily legible gay sub-texts of *Peter Grimes*, *Billy Budd*, *Owen Wingrave* and *Death in Venice*, to make the obvious comparison with Britten.[96] Lacking detailed knowledge of Poulenc's (or Cocteau's) biography, it is unlikely that the average opera-goer appreciates *La Voix humaine* for the gay *cri de cœur* that it is, and even the homoerotic dimension of *Les Biches* and *Aubade* is hesitant, repressed or, in the case of the latter, dispersed as a result of the weakness of Poulenc's scenario (see the second chapter). Nor was Poulenc any kind of sexual radical; indeed, by dying as they do, singing the 'Salve Regina' and the 'Veni Creator', the sisters of Compiègne offer themselves up as sacrificial victims for the eventual restoration of the patriarchal order of Monarchy and Church, and the power of Father and Husband is similarly reaffirmed at the end of the gender-bending mayhem of *Les Mamelles de Tirésias*. If, according to one now familiar view, classical opera is 'about' the 'undoing of women',[97] it may be that gay composers who, like Poulenc, 'project' themselves into tragic female personae are contributing to the 'undoing' – or at least to the eventual recuperation – of homosexuals as well.

When we come to the question of Poulenc's musical *style*, the situation is even more conjectural than that regarding the themes of his work. Thus far, gay musicologists have not successfully demonstrated the existence of a specifically gay compositional style, any more than feminist scholars can be said to have convincingly established the lineaments of a 'female' musical mode, as opposed to highlighting the undoubted presence of 'female', or feminist, themes in a significant number of works.[98] For the ideologically non-committed, such discussions can resemble the old debates about 'black' and 'white' jazz, now happily consigned to the musicological dustbin. Thus, on the basis of an analysis of the second movement of Schubert's Unfinished Symphony – that Schubert was gay is now plausibly assumed, though scarcely 'proven' beyond doubt – Susan McClary, by far the best scholar in the field, feels able to assert that, in contrast to Beethoven, Schubert's music 'tends to disdain goal-oriented desire per se for the sake of a sustained image of pleasure and an open, flexible sense of self' and concludes that, in this single movement at least, Schubert's compositional style 'resembles uncannily some of the narrative structures that gay writers and critics are exploring today'.[99]

But it may be that this characterisation of a 'gay' musical sensibility and style is itself deeply essentialist and hardly fits the music of Poulenc – to say nothing of that of the notably puritanical Britten or the pugnacious Tippett or, for that matter, of the music of Schubert *as a whole*. Poulenc's own style is pithy, concise, tightly structured and goal-directed to a fault, centred and organised in a way he himself never was, in sharp contrast, say, to that of the other great twentieth-century French Catholic composer, the impeccably heterosexual Olivier Messiaen (1908–92) whose diffuse, discursive, anti-teleological music Poulenc certainly admired but disliked on the whole precisely on account of what he saw as its absence of structure and direction (see C pp. 554, 592, etc.). Elsewhere, and perhaps in contradiction to her argument on Schubert, McClary has plausibly shown that almost all of the most accessible and popular – that is, in effect, tonal, tuneful and traditional – twentieth-century American composers were gay (Copland, Gershwin, Barber, Thomson, Bernstein) while, with notable exceptions (John Cage, Harry Partch, Henry Cowell), the modernist *avant-garde* was predominantly heterosexual:

> There was almost a kind of self-selection in American music. The straight boys claimed the moral high ground of modernism and fled to the universities, and the queers literally took center stage in concert halls and opera houses and ballet, all of which are musics that people are more likely to respond to.[100]

All this leads to the curious conclusion that, in America at least, the queers wrote 'straight' music for a predominantly straight musical public, while it was the straight boys on campus who, musically speaking, were 'queering the pitch' for an audience composed largely of themselves and their students. In France, it would be difficult to think of a 'straighter' composer than Poulenc, unless it be his thoroughly straight co-members of Les Six whose music was championed above all by the man (Cocteau) whom Cyril Connolly memorably described as 'one of three great homosexual trail blazers of the twentieth century'.

There remains, finally, the question of Poulenc's Catholicism and its problematic relationship to his sexuality.[101] Publicly, Poulenc could not be more positive about his religion: 'it is my greatest freedom' ('*ma plus grande liberté*'), he told his radio listeners in 1954 (ECR p. 108). Privately, however, he was rather less affirmative, though he never doubted the essential tenets of his faith nor did he question the authority of the institutional Church that embodied them. Yet much of the time Poulenc was scarcely happier in his Catholicism than he was in his homosexuality: how, given his melancholy temperament and the ingrained homophobia of the Church, could it ever have been otherwise? Sometimes, it is true, he was able to reconcile his faith and his sexuality as when, at Rocamadour in July 1957, he gave thanks to the Black Virgin ('she understands everything', C p. 873) for leading him to his new love 'Louis the builder'. But this was a rare respite from anxiety and guilt, and one finds him far more often bewailing his 'total spiritual desert' during Mass when he longs for the closing words, *Ite missa est,* to put an end to his misery, confessing how much he dreads 'intelligent priests' and how he longs for a simple-minded country *curé* who will just give him the bread and the wine that he needs (C pp. 847-9). Poulenc suffered as much through his love of God as he did through his love of the five men in his life, concluding unhappily that 'love is not a good thing for me' (C p. 888). Yet he also knew that, *precisely because it made him suffer*, love, whether it was of God, Raymonde Linossier, or of Richard, Raymond, Lucien, Louis or Claude, was the *fons et origo* of his music, and that Catholicism, though it made him suffer even more, enabled him to transfigure his suffering into art and, through the doctrine of the reversibility of merits, to contribute to the redemption of the world. 'There's no doubting that my Saintly Ladies [the 16 Carmelite sisters] wanted to purify me by fire' (C p. 809), he wrote in 1954 at the height of his personal and artistic affliction, and he took utterly seriously the novena offered by *all* the Carmelite brothers and sisters in the United States for the successful completion of the *Dialogues*, not least the elderly blind brother who 'offered up' his imminent paralysis so that Poulenc might be able to 'glorify through his music the blessed martyrs of Compiègne (see letter of Father Griffin, head of the Dallas Carmel, to Poulenc, June 1954, C pp. 795-6). Non-Catholics might scoff at the efficacy of such sacrificial self-offerings; Poulenc most emphatically did not. Throughout his life Poulenc loathed being labelled – be it 'futurist', 'cubist', 'Dadaist' or whatever (see C p. 99) – and the idea of being cast as a 'gay composer' would surely have appalled

POULENC AT NOIZAY IN THE LATE 1950S

him. His attitude was, in essence, take me or leave me, don't split me into a monk and a musical street monkey, accept me as you find me, my music, which is born of my suffering, is my portrait, so listen to it without prejudice and above all *enjoy it*.

Notes

The Parises of Francis Poulenc

1.   The present section is based on the valuable overview of 'queer Paris' by Michael D. Sibalis in David Higgs (ed.), *Queer Sites. Gay Urban Histories since 1600* (Routledge, 1999), pp. 10-37, and on Gilles Barbedette and Michel Carassou, *Paris Gay 1925* (Presses de la Renaissance, 1981), plus various primary sources, notably Julien Green, *Jeunesse* (Plon, 1974), the *Correspondance* of Henry de Montherlant and Roger Peyrefitte (Robert Laffont, 1983) and Roger Peyrefitte, *Propos secrets* (Albin Michel, 1977).

2.   Jean Genet, *Notre-Dame-des-Fleurs* (Folio, 1998), p. 102.

3.   See Green, *Jeunesse*, p. 65 and Jean Hugo, *Le Regard de la mémoire* (Actes Sud, 1983), p. 151.

4.   Peyrefitte, *Propos secrets*, p. 58.

The Ox on the Roof

5.   George Moore, *Confessions of a Young Man* (McGill-Queen's University Press, 1972), p. 102.

6.   The following account of Le Gaya and Le Boeuf sur le Toit is based principally on Maurice Sachs, *Au temps du Boeuf sur le Toit* (Grasset, 1987, first published 1939), supported by Steegmuller's biography of Cocteau and James Harding's useful *The Ox on the Roof. Scenes from Musical Life in Paris on the Twenties* (Macdonald, 1972), esp. pp. 80-5.

See also Myriam Chimènes, 'Poulenc and His Patrons: Social Convergences' in Sidney Buckland and Myriam Chimènes (eds.), *Francis Poulenc. Music, Art and Literature* (Ashgate, 1999), pp. 210-51.

7.   See Hugo, *Le Regard de la mémoire*, p. 209. For the meaning of *'couronne'*, see Montherlant and Peyrefitte, *Correspondance*, p. 42.

8.   Hugo, *Le Regard de la mémoire*, p. 210.

9.   Quoted in Steegmuller, *Cocteau*, p. 264.

10.   Hugo, *Le Regard de la mémoire*, p. 212.

11.   See Christian Gury, *L'Honneur flétri d'un évêque homosexuel en 1937* (Editions Kimé, 2000), pp. 149-50. According to Peyrefitte, the Prince-King-Duke's lovers included the one-time light heavyweight boxing champion of the world Georges Carpentier (1894-1975).

12.   Maurice Sachs, *Le Sabbat. Souvenirs d'une jeunesse orageuse* (Gallimard, 1960), p. 175. (First published 1946.)

13.   On Satie, see the hilarious and moving account in Roger Shattuck, *The Banquet Years. The Origins of the Avant-garde in France: 1885 to World War I* (Jonathan Cape, 1955). This classic work is the best possible introduction to the early modernist movement, of which Les Six's music is one of the terminal expressions.

14.   Somewhat surprisingly, Poulenc never liked jazz and denied that it had ever had any influence on his music.

15.   All quotations from Jean Cocteau, *Le Coq et l'arlequin* (Stock, 1983). For good general discussions of the music of Les Six, see Harding, *The Ox on the Roof* and Jean Roy, *Le Groupe des Six* (Seuil, 1994).

16.   Quoted by Ivry, *Francis Poulenc*, p. 23.

17. Sachs, *Au temps du Boeuf sur le Toit*, p. 234.

18. See Mellers, *Francis Poulenc*, pp. 16-23. Poulenc himself says that one of the female *pas de deux* in the ballet became in performance 'a secretly Proustian dance (Albertine and *une amie* at Balbec)' (ECR p. 54).

19. For a detailed discussion, see Sophie Robert, 'Raymonde Linossier: 'Lovely soul who was my flame''', in Buckland and Chimènes, *Francis Poulenc*, pp. 87-139.

20. For a full discussion, see Mellers, *Francis Poulenc*, pp. 24-5.

     Andrew Clements, 'Poulenc is too, too, charming', *The Guardian*, 9 January 1999.

21. Harding, *The Ox on the Roof*, p. 221. Most of the incidental details that follow are taken from pp. 220-4 of this work.

22. For a searching analysis of the musical means by which Poulenc achieves these effects, see Mellers, *Francis Poulenc*, pp. 26-32. Like Harding (*The Ox on the Roof*, pp. 223-4), Mellers (p. 32) sees *Aubade* as linked to the question of Poulenc's sexual identity. See also Ivry, *Francis Poulenc*, p. 71.

Homosexuality, Catholicism and modernism

24. See Richard Griffiths, *The Reactionary Revolution. The Catholic Revival in French Literature* (Constable, 1966), still by far the best study of the whole movement in question.

25. The following account is based primarily on Raïssa Maritain's own account in *Les Grandes Amitiés* (Descleé de Brouwer, 1949, first published 1941), supported by Jean-Luc Barré's excellent biography, *Jacques et Raïssa Maritain, Les Mendiants du ciel* (Stock, 1996). For Cocteau and Sachs, I have drawn heavily on Steegmuller's biography of Cocteau as well as on the writings of the various individuals concerned.

Only essential references are given.

26. On Ghéon's career as a homosexual and his conversion to Catholicism, see the lively account in Alan Sheridan, *André Gide*, especially pp. 195-8, 198-201 and 285-8.

27. Most of Cocteau's words quoted in the present section are taken from his *Lettre à Jacques Maritain* published in 1926. Radiguet's 'prophecy' regarding his own death is recorded in Cocteau's preface to his posthumous novel *Le Bal du comte d'Orgel* (1924).

28. See Sachs, *Le Sabbat*, p. 142.

29. Jean Bourgoint and his sister Jeanne are the models for the incestuous siblings, Paul and Elisabeth, in Cocteau's novel *Les Enfants terribles* (1929). On Christmas Eve 1929, Jeanne Bourgoint committed suicide, in emulation, it was said, of Elisabeth's self-inflicted death in the novel. Cocteau had introduced Jeanne, as well as her brother, to opium, and some people held him morally responsible for her death by encouraging her to imitate the fictional heroine she had inspired.

30. See Steegmuller, *Jean Cocteau*, p. 6 (footnote).

31. Jacques Maritain, *Réponse à Jean Cocteau* (Stock, 1993), p. 81.

32. So Steegmuller conjectures in *Jean Cocteau*, p. 357. Bourgoint who had followed Cocteau into the Church also took communion at the time.

33. Bourgoint's often moving, always interesting, letters have been published under the title of *Le Retour de l'enfant terrible* (Desclée de Brouwer, 1975), preceded by a full account of his life by Jean Mouton.

34. See Barré, *Jacques et Raïssa Maritain*, pp. 373-4.

35. Jean Desbordes, *J'adore* (Grasset, 1928), pp. 132-3. The abridged

translation quoted here is taken from Steegmuller, *Jean Cocteau*, p. 390.

36.   Quoted in Barré, *Jacques et Raïssa Maritain*, p. 375.

37.   Quoted in Steegmuller, *Jean Cocteau*, p. 390.

38.   Quotations from Barré, *Jacques et Raïssa Maritain*, pp. 375-7.

39.   Jean Cocteau, *Le Livre blanc* (Passage du Marais, 1992), p. 85. On Cambacérès, see the note on homosexual legislation in France above.

40.   On Desbordes's death, see Steegmuller, Jean Cocteau, pp. 447-9. Cocteau's wartime record is discussed briefly in the fifth chapter, 'Faith, death and freedom: Poulenc's music 1937-50'.

41.   The present section is based on Sachs's own account in *Le Sabbat*, supported by Steegmuller, *Jean Cocteau* and Jean-Michel Belle, *Les Folles Anneés de Maurice Sachs* (Grasset, 1979).

42.   The best account of this episode is in Barré, *Jacques et Raïssa Maritain*, pp. 329-34. Not surprisingly, Sachs himself denied the whole business.

43.   Interestingly, his partner-in-crime was Violette Leduc (1907-72), the acclaimed lesbian author of the autobiographical *La Bâtarde* (1964).

44.   Max Jacob, *La Défense de Tartuffe* (Gallimard, 1964, first published 1919), p. 162.

45.   Julien Green, *Jeunesse* (Plon, 1974), p. 215 (Green's italics).

46.   Julien Green, *Le Malfaiteur*, in *Ouevres complètes*, III, ed. Jacques Petit (Gallimard, 1973), p. 302.

47.   Ibid., p. 322.

48.   On the ramifications of this well-known 'case', see the superbly documented study by Gury, *L'Honneur flétri d'un évêque homosexuel en 1937*.

49.   As it happens, the most accomplished French Catholic boys' choir of the time, the *Petits chanteurs à la croix de bois*, was directed by a well-known homosexual priest, the Abbé Maillet (1896-1963) and did have a significant gay 'following' (see Gury, *L'Honneur flétri*, pp. 132-3). Poulenc knew Maillet well (C 467): it was he who commissioned the *Quatre motets pour un temps de pénitence* for performance by his choir in 1939.

50.   Sachs, *Le Sabbat*, pp. 70-1.

51.   This is Christopher Robinson's summary of Merle's argument in his much recommended *Scandal in the Ink. Male and Female Homosexuality in Twentieth-century French Literature* (Cassell, 1995), p. 75.

52.   Green, *Jeunesse*, p. 146.

53.   Jacob, *La Défense de Tartuffe*, pp. 197-8.

54.   Letter of 12 April 1927, in Max Jacob/Jean Cocteau, *Correspondance 1917-1944* (Editions Paris-Méditerraneé, 2000), p. 529.

55.   Desbordes, *J'adore*, p. 54.

56.   Jean Genet, *Notre-Dame-des-Fleurs* (Folio, 1998), p. 89. To make the gender-bending criss-cross of images even more telling, when Divine is arrested while drunkenly singing the 'Veni Creator' on the boulevards, she faints and is revived by the *gendarmes*' fanning her with their handkerchiefs, like so many 'Holy Women who were wiping my face, my Divine Face' (*'Ils étaient les Saintes Femmes qui m'essuyaient la face. Ma Divine Face'*), p. 82.

57.   See Ivry, *Francis Poulenc*, p. 89.

58.   Hugo, *Le Regard de la mémoire*, p. 440.

59.   In conversation with Claude Rostand, Poulenc says that he had 'a veritable cult' for Clemenceau in 1917 (ECR p.107). As President of the Republic between 1899 and 1906, Loubet was responsible for setting Dreyfus free and for breaking off diplomatic relations with the Vatican in 1905. Bourdet, it might be added, was gay and was rumoured to have been the lover of the leading Catholic novelist, François Mauriac.

60.   See Jane F. Fulcher, 'The Preparation for Vichy: Anti-Semitism in French Musical Culture Between the Two World Wars', *Musical Quarterly*, 79, 3 (1995), pp. 458-75.

61.   A recording of selected works by Ferroud played by the Orchestre National de Lyon under Emmanuel Krivine is available on Audivis V4810.

Black Virgin: Poulenc at Rocamadour (August 1936)

62.   Pierre Bernac and Yvonne Gouverné, *Poulenc et Rocamadour* (Zodiaque, 1974). Quoted from B 415.

63.   The present account is based on the standard work on the subject, Marie Durand-Lefebvre, *Etude sur l'origine des vierges noires* (G. Durassié, 1937), and Sophie Cassagnes-Brouquet, *Vierges noires* (Editions du Rouergue, 2000). Poulenc recounts the story of Saint Amadour/Zacchaeus in ECR 108-9.

64.   Apuleius, *The Golden Ass*, trans. Robert Graves (Penguin, 1972), pp. 22-89 (abridged).

65.   Ivry, *Francis Poulenc*, p. 90.

66.   Quoted from the accompanying notes to the EMI recording (7243 566837 2) of Francis Poulenc, *Concertos, musique symphonique et religieuse*. The battle referred to is that of Las Navas de Tolosa (1212) in which the banner of Notre-Dame de Rocamadour is said to have

brought a French force victory over the Moors.

67. Jean Cocteau, *Portraits-souvenirs* (1935), quoted in Jean-Marie Magnan, *Cocteau* (Descleé de Bouwer, 1968), p. 53.

68. Jean Cocteau, *Le Rappel à l'ordre* (1926), quoted in ibid., p. 48.

69. When in the creative throes of 'giving birth' to *Dialogues des Carmélites*, Poulenc described himself as being 'obnubilated' by his subject (C p. 766); the parallel with the 'obombrabit' ('the power of the Highest shall overshadow thee') of Luke 1: 35 is quite striking.

70. Significantly, it was in the anxious summer of 1938 that Poulenc began working on his gender-bending opera *Les Mamelles de Tirésias*. No less interesting is the fact that, around the same time, he considered writing an opera based on Balzac's lesbian novelette *La Fille aux yeux d'or* (1835), obviously attracted by the possibility – as well as put off by the difficulty – of treating the 'inversion theme' (his words, C p. 446) openly.

Faith, death and freedom: Poulenc's music 1937-50

71. Mellers, *Francis Poulenc*, p. 75.

72. See ECR pp. 110-11, where the Mass in G is explicitly described as 'romane', in contrast to the later, and grander, *Stabat Mater* (1951) which is said to be 'Jesuit' in its style.

73. Mellers, *Francis Poulenc*, p. 79.

74. All quotations from J pp. 21-1. The Grand Charteuse is a Carthusian monastery located in the French Alps near Saint-Laurent-du-Port between Grenoble and Chambéry. For a detailed and insightful discussion of the whole cycle, see Sidney Buckland, '"The coherence of opposites": Eluard, Poulenc and the poems of *Tel jour telle nuit*', in Buckland and Chimènes (eds.), *Francis Poulenc*, pp. 145-77.

75. On Cocteau and Brecker, see Steegmuller, *Jean Cocteau*, pp. 443-4. The Guitry story is told in Arthur King Peters, *Jean Cocteau and His World* (Thames and Hudson, 1987), p. 141. A bust of Cocteau by Brecker stands on a pedestal above Cocteau's tomb in the chapel of Saint-Blaise-des-Simples at Milly-la-Forêt south of Paris.

76. Another prominent gay Vichyist was the *académicien* Abel Hermant, familiarly (if untranslatably) known as 'La Belle au Bois d'Hermant' (*la belle au bois dormant* = Sleeping Beauty, see Gury, *L'Honneur Flétri d'un évêque homosexuel en 1937*, pp. 81, 111 etc.).

77. Words and translations form Felicity Lott's recital *Le Voyage à Paris* (Hyperion A 66147).

78. A private performance was given at the Paris home of Marie-Laure de Noailles in late 1943 or early 1944, in the presence of Eluard and the work's dedicatee, Picasso.

79. The figure of Tirésias, 'old man with wrinkled female breasts' (T. S. Eliot, *The Waste Land*), has exercised a fascination in the twentieth-century artistic imagination, not least the homosexual imagination. In *Tirésias* (1954), Marcel Jouhandeau used the bisexual seer as the central figure of his hymn to anal intercourse ('I am certainly a man but I am a woman too,' *Tirésias* (Arléa, 1988, p. 23), and Cocteau's reworking of the Oedipus myth, *La Machine infernale* (1934) gave a particular prominence to Tirésias; interestingly, Poulenc was considering it as a possible text for a new opera in 1959 (C pp. 909, 915). Finally, the possibly bisexual Constant Lambert, a great admirer of Poulenc, composed a ballet on the Tirésias theme in 1951.

Monologues and dialogues: Poulenc's later music 150-63

80. Gertrud von Le Fort, *Aufzeichnungen und Erinnerungen* (Benziger Verlag, 1956), p. 95. For a detailed discussion of the origins and theology of the opera, see Claude Gendre, '*Dialogues des Carmélites*: the historical

background, literary destiny and genesis of the opera', in Buckland and Chimenes (eds.), *Francis Poulenc*, pp. 274-319.

81. Georges Bernanos, *Dialogues des Carmélites* (Seuil, 1996), p. 57. Where Bernanos's words are, as here, put to music by Poulenc, I have used the translation by Joseph Machlis of the opera's libretto (Milan: Ricordi, 1981); the present extract is on p. 111. All other translations are my own.

82. On the complex dispute with Emmet Lavery (who had purchased stage rights to Le Fort's novelle when he wrote his own play *The Last on the Scaffold*), see Buckland (ed.), *Francis Poulenc*, pp. 391-2.

83. See, for example, Mellers, *Francis Poulenc*, p. 127.

84. Elsewhere he added that 'if Mozart's name is absent, it is because one cannot dedicate anything to God the Father' (quoted in Daniel, *Francis Poulenc*, p. 300).

85. Poulenc, 'Comment j'ai composé les *Dialogues des Carmélites*', in *L'Opéra de Paris* 14 (1957), quoted in Daniel, *Francis Poulenc*, p. 300.

86. See Mellers, *Francis Poulenc*, p. 128. For a detailed discussion of *La Voix humaine*, see Denis Walecx, '"A musical confession": Poulenc, Cocteau and *La Voix humaine*', in Buckland and Chimènes (eds.), *Francis Poulenc*, pp. 320-47.

87. Poulenc described La *Voix humaine* as his *'Dialogues avec un sergent'* (i.e. Louis) (C p. 863). He also had another 'gentil boyfriend' during this period, a 28-year-old junior executive at Citroën named Claude (see C p. 874).

88. Cocteau was as obsessed by strangling as Poulenc was by decapitation, originally as a result of Isadora Duncan's death in 1927, strangled when her scarfe became caught in the wheel of the sports car she was driving on the Promenade des Anglais in Nice. Michaël in *Les Enfants terribles* is killed in this way.

89.   Mellers, *Francis Poulenc*, pp. 136-7.

90.   Pierre Bernac, *Francis Poulenc. The Man and his Songs*, trans. Winifred Radford (Gollancz, 1977), p. 29. The original comparison to Gilles was made by the music critic Paul Guth.

91.   Julia Kristeva, '*Le Christ mort de Holbein*', in *Soleil noir. Dépression et mélancolie* (Folio/Gallimard, 1990), p. 128.

92.   François Mauriac, *Le Nouveau Bloc-Notes 1961-64* (Flammarion, 1968), p. 242. I owe this reference to Machart, *Poulenc*, p. 5.

Conclusion

93.   Ivry, *Francis Poulenc*, p. 13.

94.   Rorem's magnificent *Paris Diary* (first published 1966) is essential reading on the gay and artistic 'scene' in 1950s Paris. His own song style is strongly influenced by Poulenc's and his commemorative song 'Francis Poulenc', to a text by Frank O'Hara, is the best possible tribute to the art of his master.

95.   Or, to be more precise, his principal *male* musical influences, though there is some evidence that Wanda Landowska (1879-1959), if not Nadia Boulanger (1887-1979), was bisexually orientated. The standard sources are silent on the question of Bernac's sexuality, and there were, of course, rumours of a homosexual relationship between composer and singer, which Poulenc convincingly scotches in a letter of December 1953 (see C p. 772).

96.   For an admirable summary of homosexual themes in Britten's operas, see Michael Wilcox, *Benjamin Britten's Operas* (Absolute Press, 1997).

97.   See Catherine Clément, *Opera, or the Undoing of Women*, trans. Betsy Wing (Virago, 1989).

98.   For a stimulating and representative collection of essays written from a
      gay musicological perspective, see Philip Brett, Elizabeth Wood and
      Gary C. Thomas (eds.), *Queering the Pitch. The New Gay and Lesbian
      Musicology* (Routledge, 1994). For a useful summary of contemporary
      feminist approaches to musical style, see Nicholas Cook, *Music. A Very
      Short Introduction* (Oxford University Press, 1998), pp. 112-25.

99.   Quoted from Cook, *Music*, p. 114.

100. Quoted in Howard Pollack, *Aaron Copland. The Life and Works of an
      Uncommon Man* (Faber, 1999), p. 525.

101. It was only after completing this book that I read Mark D. Jordan's riveting
      The Silence of Sodom. Homosexuality in Modern Catholicism (University of
      Chicago Press, 2000). Though Jordan's argument is concerned essentially
      with the Catholic clergy, much of what he says regarding 'clerical camp'
      and 'liturgy queens' (pp. 179-198) as well as the centrality of the Body of
      Christ in gay catholicism (pp. 203-8), could be applied to the gay French
      Catholics discussed here, though not always to Poulenc himself.

Picture credits

All photographs reproduced with the kind permission of Mme Rosine
Seringe, except: page 18, courtesy of Roger-Viollet; page 64, © Combier
Imprimeur; page 68, © R. Delon/Castelet; and pages 110, 112 and 116,
courtesy of Cliché Bibliothèque nationale de France, Paris. The publishers
would like to thank Mme Rosine Seringe for her help.

Outlines

Chronicling the lives of some of the most exceptional gay and lesbian artists of the last century.

1-899791-55-8   *David Hockney* by Peter Adam
1-899791-70-1   *Bessie Smith* by Jackie Kay
1-899791-60-4   *Benjamin Britten* by Michael Wilcox
1-899791-71-X   *Arthur Rimbaud* by Benjamin Ivry
1-899791-61-2   *Federico García Lorca* by David Johnston
1-899791-47-7   *k.d. lang* by Rose Collis
1-899791-37-X   *Armistead Maupin* by Patrick Gale
1-899791-42-6   *Tallulah Bankhead* by Bryony Lavery
1-899791-66-3   *We are Michael Field* by Emma Donoghue
1-899791-48-5   *Quentin Crisp* by Tim Fountain
1-899791-09-4   *Francis Poulenc* by Richard D. E. Burton

1-899791-73-6   *Morrissey* by Pat Reid (new for 2003)
1-899791-68-X   *Pedro Almodovar* by David Johnston (new for 2003)
1-899791-43-4   *Ziggy Stardust* by Richard Smith (new for 2003)

Available from all good bookstores or orders directly to Absolute Press. Send cheques (payable to Absolute Press) or VISA/Mastercard details to: Absolute Press, Scarborough House, 29 James Street West, Bath BA1 2BT. Phone 01225 316 013 for any further details or visit the website at www.absolutepress.demon.co.uk